THE STORY OF SHE

An Anthology of *Her* Perspective

THE STORY OF SHE

An
Anthology
of *Her* Perspective

DORIS PUSHPAM

Buon-Cattivi Press

Adelaide, Australia

Published by the Buon-Cattivi Press. 2022
Adelaide, Australia

ISBN (PAPERBACK): 978-1-922314-05-5
ISBN (EBOOK): 978-1-922314-06-2

Editing by Cameron Rutherford.
Cover art and book design
by Andrew Crooks.

For my parents, Selva and Doreen
who allowed me to be me
and loved me for it.

ABOUT THE AUTHOR

Hailing from the humid, windy, sometimes scorching suburbs of Malaysia, Doris Pushpam chose to pursue the ever-promising path of creative writing. When she isn't making questionable life decisions she can be found embroidering, baking, painting, losing chess games to her father, reading, journaling, playing video games, or picking up some new hobby. Sometimes she creates worlds where women are able to tell their story and other times she writes in rhyme and lives in the clouds. She enjoys creating chaos and happily-ever-afters and nothing makes her happier than that final full stop and a perfect rhyme. Doris Pushpam is currently undertaking a PhD in Creative Writing (in line with her tendency for making questionable life decisions) through which she hopes to continue advocating for women in oppressed cultures. In her previous research she explored the notion of becoming a woman in relation to the oral tradition, investigated the many nuances of change that affect women from oppressed cultures, and also discussed the need for women to form a space where all aspects of oneself that one chooses to be, can exist. She is inspired by the works of Simone de Beauvoir, Jane Austen, Gloria Anzaldúa, Maya Angelou, and Sylvia Plath.

ACKNOWLEDGEMENTS

My cornucopia of thanks flows to:

My father, who assiduously goes through each line of every first draft. My stories are better because of you.

My mother, who was there for me in times of stress when the things in my head would not materialise on a page. You were gracious in putting up with my foul moods.

Brian, Daphne, and Joachim, who I use to bounce my ideas off. Thank you for putting up with my hours of rambling.

Dr Alex Dunkin, who is as great a lecturer as he is an editor-publisher. My interest in and love for short fiction was first realised in your classroom with *Talia*.

Mr Mark Auger, who was there for the first poem I ever wrote and unlocked my creative writing passion through his enthusiastic teaching and constant encouragement.

Dr Amelia Walker, who tirelessly provides guidance and support, pushing me toward opportunities such as this one.

The Creative Writing team at UniSA for nurturing my passion in this field and for all their support during my undergraduate studies.

The 2014-2015 teaching staff of the Canadian International Matriculation Programme at Sunway College, Malaysia.

Last but not least, my great grandma, Pushpam Jothy, whose life is an inspiration for me to be all that I can be. I wish you were still here to read this with your magnifying glass.

Dear Reader,

I wrote this series of stories as a vestibule into the maze that is a woman. This book stemmed from frustration at how things remain the same no matter how hard we fight for change. Through these stories I outline the life and times of the many women in my life: those I have met in passing, those I have never met at all, those I have loved, and those I have lost. This book is an ode to their existence.

Divided into three chapters, each story tells of different aspects of a woman's being. The first chapter, *Retrospect*, features protagonists that have already lived through the struggle. We follow them as they tell us their story. In the second chapter, *Introspect*, we meet her at the start of her tale and encounter with her the horrors and joys that lie ahead. The last chapter, titled *Prospect*, consists of stories exploring what could happen to her if things continue as they are.

It is my ardent wish that as you peruse the pages of this anthology, you put yourself in her shoes and consider *her* perspective. More importantly, I hope you see why there is a need for change and how to go about exacting it in your own little way through small actions to create a ripple of change. It is time to break the cycle. It is time to do more to change *her* story.

Doris,
Woman, Feminist, Dreamer.

CONTENTS

RETROSPECT

Musings of a Girl in a Tree   *13*

Story of My Life   *19*

Henna Stains   *26*

The Story of She   *39*

Fishes and Promises   *45*

The Tragedy of Tortoise Shells   *53*

Existence Precedes Essence   *62*

Snow White and Tar Black   *70*

Cotton Candy Clouds and Graveyard Stars   *77*

Talia   *82*

The Conditioned Smile   *86*

She is Clay   *90*

INTROSPECT

The Sin of Skin   *97*

The Runaway Bride   *103*

Monsters in the Moonlight   *110*

Growing Jasmines   *116*

Just Another Day in May   *126*

This is a Short Story   *130*

She Unravels   *133*

The Curse of an Empty Nest   *137*

The Paradox of Porcelain Hearts   146
Loud Minds and Quiet People   150
Ode to Sarees   157
Creating Constellations   161
The Many Nuances of Silence   173

PROSPECT

The Variety Store   185
Justice is Sweet   192
If We Were Bees   198
Choose Your Fate   204

RETROSPECT

On knowing now
what I didn't know then

MUSINGS OF A GIRL IN A TREE

I wonder where I would be today if it wasn't for all the women in my life. Maybe I would have become the ornithologist or aviculturist I wanted to be. I could have been an apiarist and made friends with bees while collecting their honey. Baking always called my name and I always loved dancing. I remember wanting to be a data analyst when I was learning statistics in school. I learned how to make floral arrangements in school and I enjoyed that. Maybe I could have been a florist. I remember thinking I could be a better teacher than the one I had then and maybe I could have. I think maybe I would even have become the accountant they wanted me to be. I don't really know what I would have chosen if I had the chance but I know one thing. I know that I would at least be somewhere better than where I am now. Not hung by a saree on the branch of an aged jackfruit tree, swinging in the westward bound winds, hoping death would come quicker.

While I am still present let's discuss how I got here. I think you will find the story interesting, if nothing else. I did tell you that the women in my life are the reason I am where I am. I always had a feeling that they would be the culprits. I didn't think they would cause my death but I did know that they would play a hand in making my life miserable. Some may blame fate for what befell me but I know they were the reason. Let us start with the woman who probably wished I was dead many times since I was young.

Now, I don't want to make assumptions about my mother but I think she always hated me. I don't know when her dislike started but I did feel love from her a long time ago then nothing at all. I of course have my reasons for believing that she hates me. Maybe if I talk it out with you, you can help me understand or determine if it is all in my head.

My mother was one of those women who called the shots in the household. My father may have believed that he was in charge but she could manipulate anyone to do her will. Everyone except me. I think that is what she despised. Her manipulation never worked on me. She could cry on cue, play the victim and make a racket wherever she was until she got what she wanted. I never fell for the tears. I used to roll my eyes as those around me bowed to her every wish. She found a way around my so-called impertinence by making those around me carry out her punishment. I remember an instance when my brother hit me with a broomstick because she had complained that I was being disrespectful to her. She had bombarded him with complaints and tears until she made her anger his. He hit me till bits of my skin stuck to the rattan stick. He only stopped when my father stepped in.

My brother was never temperamental. He never raised his voice and tended to keep to himself. She pushed him to hit me. That woman carried tales about me to my father and I could tell when she did because he would try to advise me about how to behave. She made sure that he was always on her side by making sure that her side of the story was all that he heard. I never had a chance in that house. I didn't even have a chance outside the house because she and her friends would meet and discuss all the ways I was letting her down. She let them mock me and chastise me when I was barely ten years old. I did everything I could to get away from her. This is the result of my efforts. I guess she won in the end. I think I am right in saying that she always hated me. I think you would agree with me on that by the end of this if you haven't been convinced thus far.

The next culprit is my grandmother. She is not so different from my mother. She did raise my mother after all. My grandmother is a vain woman. She belittled my mother every chance she got and when I was born I was told that she took an instant dislike towards me because I didn't look like her. I think my mother learned how to be manipulative from her. My grandmother played her game a little differently. She made those around her pity her and in turn they felt compelled to do things for her. She used her tears too and when it suited her she lied about all the misfortunes in her life. She was the reason my mother had arranged a marriage match for me. I was walking home from school with the neighbour's son and my grandmother had seen. She was particular about caste so she did her research on him. When she found out that he was from a different caste than us, she had thrown a tantrum.

'I should kill myself before they get married so I don't have to see what this family becomes. We will be a disgrace,' she said.

No one listened when I said that I wasn't even dating the boy. She cried and pulled at her hair, slapping herself and cursing anyone who dared try to comfort her. She only shut up when my father told her that he would arrange a marriage with a boy of her choice to make sure that the bloodline remained pure. I think all that endogamy must have made them all a little more insane. As insane as she was, her manipulation worked. My mother and her arranged a match and they were the reason I ran. I guess I am fortunate that I won't be alive long enough to be anything like either of them. I'd choose death over that any day.

It isn't fair of me to only blame the two of them. It was the other women who contributed to the whole situation who also share the blame. These women were my neighbours, my mother's and my grandmother's friends and in-laws, my aunts, and my cousins. They were all raised the same. They followed the same rules that they once despised. They were as tortured as me but they seemed to like it. Maybe it was only me who saw our traditions as oppression. I used to think they were good at faking it or maybe they were beaten into submission but they all just seemed resigned to a life of being controlled by the matriarch before them. They seemed to relish the thought that one day it would be them calling the shots, dictating how others like them live their lives, and dishing out the same punishments they were given. These women didn't know me. They knew what my mother and my grandmother told them about me. Every argument I had with my mother reached them and they didn't hold back when they told me off. When I dared tell them that they had no right to correct me, I was greeted with my father's belt the moment I entered the house. I think without them there, I would have gotten away. The cyclical abuse that they receive and pass on needs to go but I don't think I have time to fix a system so broken. I can only remove myself from their teachings and tradition, not willingly in this case, but at least I can proudly say that I played no part in any of it.

I am not angry with them. I think I am just a little bit disappointed in them. These women have some semblance of control in their lives and they chose to control other women. They didn't try to change our story. All their stories start with abuse and end with abuse, passing on the baton to the next generation with pride. They chased after me when I ran, ordering their sons and husbands to catch me. When they did, my mother had slapped me and spat in my face before the other women began to attack. They didn't hesitate. They didn't hold back. I felt my spine crack as they stepped on me with their sandals and when I couldn't stand, they brought a saree and used it to hang me from the oldest tree in the village. My grandmother's smile is fresh in my mind as they hit me with sticks and threw stones at me. She didn't do a thing. She was probably happy that I didn't defile our bloodline. My mother was the same. There were no tears shed though I know she will put on a show later when she cries about how she had to do the things she did to raise me right. They will all fall for it too.

I think if I had a chance I could change things. I would have stopped the abuse. I would have loved my daughter. I would have taught her that the traditions we have are antiquated and shouldn't have existed in the first place. I would have made her my friend instead of the bane of my existence. I would have let her explain herself before I lost my head and I wouldn't have used the ways of my mother and my grandmother to get what I want. I would have let her marry who she wanted and she wouldn't have had to run away to escape her fate. She wouldn't be where I am, with a cracked spine slowly puncturing my lungs as I happily give in to death because in death I will be free of all of them.

You might say that maybe I shouldn't have run, that maybe if I stayed and went through with the wedding, I could have changed things. You may be right if you were dealing with people who would listen. My fate was sealed even before my grandmother shed her first fake tear. I would have been killed a little later but killed nevertheless unless I abided by their rules and followed their traditions. It is not a life I want to live. Maybe in my next life I will be fortunate enough not to be born a woman because then I could be the ornithologist or aviculturist I wanted to be. I could be an apiarist, befriending the bees while stealing their honey. I could bake and dance, analyse all the data I want till I go blind or I could make the prettiest floral arrangements and sell them for exorbitant prices. I could be a better teacher than the ones I've had because they only taught me that being a woman means being nothing at all. I could have been more than nothing. Instead my story ends here with a saree and a jackfruit tree, with a spine that finally gives way as the sun dies on my last day.

STORY OF MY LIFE

I have lost a lot of things in my ninety years of life. I don't really misplace them, they just sort of disappear. I lost my favourite broach, the only thing I had left from my mother. I lost my wedding bangles and I can't remember if I ever had a wedding ring. I lost my parents at fifteen, the same year I lost my virginity and I lost my husband not long after the birth of my ninth child. Then I lost the first of my nine children at sixty-eight. Recently I have begun to lose my memories. Before I lose my life, here is my story.

I was a young bride at fifteen, a sickly orphan whose property was stolen by relatives. They married me off to a widower twice my age so that I wouldn't be their responsibility any longer. They assumed I would die because I was always ill but I didn't. Somehow I lived.

My husband was not a cruel man. He was mild-mannered and I liked having him around. He didn't demand things from me. He left me alone for the most part at the beginning of our marriage. He didn't say much initially but as we got to know each other I grew to love him. I had my first child at fifteen, a boy. The following year it was a girl. It was the same the year after. I even had a pair of twins. I had my ninth and last child when I was twenty-six. A year later I lost my husband.

Those around me didn't hesitate to try to find me

another husband. Men would come knocking in the pretence of checking on me and they would touch and grab and try to take but I didn't let them. I saw the way they looked at my young daughters and I made up my mind. At twenty-six I decided that I will raise my children alone. That was when I began to bind.

I bound my body with cotton towels, the same towels I used as diapers for my children. Each morning before I headed to the market, I would tuck one part of the towel under my armpit and hold it down while I wrapped my breasts twice over with the rest of the towel. Then I would put on the loosest blouse I owned. I tied my hair in a low bun and kept my eyes down whenever I left the house. My eldest son would follow me and I would tell my eldest daughter to keep an eye on the other children. They got used to the routine. I did too.

My days were filled with cooking and then educating my children. I taught them how to read and write. I was fortunate enough to have parents who cared about education and in spite of my deteriorating health they ensured that I kept up with all the other children. I decided that I would do the same for my children. It was no easy feat raising nine children. There was never enough food but they didn't know that. I had to sew their uniforms for school but they never complained. It was a tiring job but a rewarding one because they always managed to make me laugh. I saw parts of my husband in each of them and I missed him from time to time. There were also times when I hated him for leaving me alone but those times were rare.

Even with all the precautions the house visits didn't stop. They brought groceries and waited around as if expecting some sort of payment. I knew what they wanted but I pretended like I didn't. My faux ignorance saved me. I learned that by being straightforward and asking them what they want, they would leave faster. After all, which man would be brave enough to say that he came over to grab my breast or pinch my thigh so hard that it leaves a dent? For the men that did dare to cross the line, my sons were there to stop them. Though they were young, they knew how to scream. No one likes a scene, so they would leave and I would reward my boys with sweets.

Knowing how to read men saved my life and the lives of my daughters. They weren't very hard to read. They spoke with their eyes and let their eyes linger on the things they wanted. They took the barest sight of skin as an invitation. They are so quick to blame you for their actions and thoughts, calling you a slut and telling their wives how you came on to them. Their wives were all gullible or maybe they just wanted to believe that their husbands weren't like those men they meet in the market that stand too close and accidentally brush against them. They were so wrong but I think they were content with being wrong because the alternative was knowing what disgusting men their husbands were.

It wasn't a healthy routine by any means but I did what I had to do. After just months of binding my breasts, I began to get rashes and then the backaches began. After a year, I had to get ointment for my nipples as they were chapped from the friction from the cloth. I wanted to remove the bindings the moment I got home but I couldn't because I wasn't sure if anyone would be stopping by. It was only at night that my breasts could breathe.

I believed it would get easier when my children were older but with age came a lot more complications. At thirty-three I was forced to marry off one of my daughters. She was seventeen at the time. I know she wasn't happy with what I did but I didn't have a choice. I knew I had to act when one day my youngest daughter came home with bloodied knees and a ripped pinafore. She had barely gotten away from the drunkard. I could no longer keep them safe. I needed help.

Looking back, I shouldn't have done what I did because she was miserable and she made her children miserable too. The man I gave her to was not the right one for her or anyone for that matter. In my haste to ensure their safety, I ignored my instincts and she paid for it. I wish I held off a little longer but the men were crowding and pushing their way in and I had to keep her and my other daughters safe.

Having a man in the house helped but it also came with another problem. He may have kept the men out but I couldn't trust him with my other daughters. I knew I had to get my daughter and him their own place or sooner or later something terrible would happen. I sold what little of my wedding jewellery I had and made him pay the remainder for a house that was close by. I was sad to see my daughter go but I think she was relieved to leave and have her own space.

At thirty-five I had my first grandchild. My daughter didn't bring the baby around much. I don't think she ever really forgave me for what I did to her. To this day she still complains about her husband and I don't think she was as fortunate as me to ever learn to love her husband. She hated him to his dying day, though I think she loved the children they had together.

With my grandchildren I had many firsts. I walked to

their house each morning and took them to kindergarten. When they were old enough for primary school I did the same. I carried them on my back and they told me stories I could never wrap my head around. They were always happy and carefree and it made me feel like maybe the world wasn't such a bad place. I was with them as they grew older. They stopped by my place after school and I would have lunch ready for them. We watched TV together and they followed the serial dramas I used to watch. When it was time to pray they would gather at the altar next to me and recite the prayers by heart. Seeing them made me believe that God really does have a plan.

My children were all grown up by then. They got jobs and settled down. They had their heartaches but they did have moments of pure bliss. They shared both with me. When I lost my husband I never believed that I could raise the children on my own. They were the only reason I didn't kill myself. I stayed alive because I knew I was the only person who would love them and give them almost everything they wanted. I also lived in fear that I would kill them. I didn't know much about raising children and my husband was a great support. In the years that I was fortunate enough to be with him, he kept the children occupied and out of trouble, did chores without me having to ask, and he even tried to cook. I didn't let him into the kitchen after the first attempt. With him I had it all: a husband, a teammate, a friend. Without him I almost gave up. I'm glad I didn't. I'm glad I stayed alive.

There were moments throughout my life when I wished that I was dead. The worst was when I lost my son. He was in a hit and run. He was only forty-five. He was a quiet boy and an even quieter man. He walked me to church each Sunday and kept me company after work. It didn't seem fair that I lived past fifty and he didn't even have a chance to reach that milestone. I cursed God for the first time that day. I asked him why he didn't take me. I watched my baby lowered into a grave wishing that I could go with him.

My health wasn't great during that time. I don't think it ever was. I didn't have enough money to go to the clinic to check when I was younger but I felt all the aches and sudden sharp pains. I knew it probably only worsened over time. I was afraid to check because I knew what I would see. My children had to drag me to the hospital and when I did meet the doctor, he prescribed me a long list of medications. The lack of food for years meant that I was malnourished and my heart wasn't doing too great either. The worst thing though was the state of my breasts. I was never kind to them. The last time I used my breasts was to feed my ninth child. That was the last time I even saw them. At seventy-five I never had a chance to put on a bra. Having small breasts when I was younger meant that I didn't need to. The moment I hit puberty I lost my parents and I didn't have a chance to ask for a bra then either. I think it would have been a little insensitive if I did. Then I got pregnant and I used my breasts for milk. I didn't think that I needed a bra. When the binding began I treated my breasts like they were a sin. I ignored the pus that oozed from my nipples and I only tightened the towels when I felt any pain. I had lost so much already at that point so I felt nothing as I added my breasts to the list.

I am ninety now and the list of things I have lost and continue to lose only seems to grow. I am losing my sight as I write this and I feel myself slip away at times. What brings me back is the sound of my great-grandchildren when they come to visit me in a house that one of my daughters bought me. They make me feel young. When they are near I have no concept of time. I am back to the seventeen-year-old mother I was and I play with them like I did with my children. I do puzzles with them and they tell me stories like my children and grandchildren used to. When they are gone I ache all over but I am happy. I keep talking about things I have lost but the things I have gained far outweigh the losses. I am looked after well and I am surrounded by family. It is a nice change from feeling alone all my young life. I wish I could tell that fifteen-year-old sickly orphan that it all worked out in the end. It was her strength that got me this far and I love her for it. I feel my life slip away day by day but I don't mind. I am ready to go.

HENNA STAINS

~

The journey of a thousand stains began with a single seed. It was purchased from a prestigious nursery that sold the most unique tropical seeds and plants. It was stored in a container in a dark room where the sun couldn't get to it. It waited for the day it would finally sprout.

The day came not two months later and it was removed from the container it was in. Paper towels were laid out and doused with water. Then the seed was placed onto the wet towels along with a dozen other seeds. The paper towels were folded in two and put in an air-tight bag before being placed in the refrigerator. After four days the bag was placed in direct sunlight where germination began.

It grew its first inch on that damp paper towel and was eventually transferred to a pot with five other seedlings that had survived their first hurdle. In the pot it was watered every three days and every time it rained the pot was brought inside so that the seedlings wouldn't drown. It grew its first thorns, then leaves, then buds. It was coated with fertiliser and wilted leaves were trimmed away to make way for new ones. It was the same for two years until the seedling became a flowering shrub.

It was then that it was stripped of its leaves. The leaves were ground into a paste and the plant was left aside to grow again. The paste or henna was black and grainy and it left a brownish-red stain on anything it got in contact with. The paste was packed in piping bags and was sold to a house in the middle of town where the eldest daughter of a farmer was to be married. She was not a young bride. She was about thirty but there was no discrimination when it came to henna. It was for celebrations and on the happiest day of a girl's life, she was adorned with it. They snipped the tip of the piping bag and drew the most intricate designs on the back of her hands, on her palms and on her feet. She was told to sit for hours with the paste on so that the design would stay on longer. They said that the longer the henna stayed on, the longer her marriage would last.

She sat at the patio of her house for hours before finally washing it off. Brownish red stains decorated her skin when she was done. There were lotus flowers on the back of her hands to represent grace and beauty. There were leaves and vines on her fingers and paisley patterns on her feet for fertility. The hours of sitting that she had done as others drew on her seemed worth it when she saw how it turned out. Though she liked the intricate patterns, she wasn't satisfied with them. As an artist, she could see that there was room for more. She liked lotus flowers but they weren't her favourite. She had seen the patterns on her skin on so many others and she wanted to be different.

So, she picked up the piping bag and added patterns of her own. She had seen it done to many other brides before her and she had always wanted to try but no one ever let her because she could ruin the design. She started by adding more leaves to her wrist. Her hands were not steady so the first few were a mess but henna is forgiving and all she had to do was wipe it away before it could stain. After leaves she tried branches and then, pulling up her skirt, she began to draw trees and birds on her ankles and calves. Her hands may not have been steady but the patterns were beautiful. Not as beautiful as her paintings that they sold in the marketplace but they were better than any henna pattern she had ever seen.

She slept in the henna and the next morning when she washed away the dye, they fell off like scabs. The patterns that were left behind were more vibrant than the ones she had before. She was proud of them and showed them to her sisters who asked her to draw on them too. She spent the eve of her wedding with her sisters, drawing birds and reminiscing.

At the sound of the temple bells they rose the next morning. They only had a few hours of sleep but knew if they slept in there was a risk that they wouldn't be in time for the main ceremony. Being late would doom the marriage. The universe would ensure that. The people would ensure that.

It was easy to shake off sleep. It is not every day that you get to don a saree the price of a horse and put on jewellery that added pounds to your neck and ears. The bangles on her wrist jingled along with her anklets and kept them all wide awake. They put on their makeup together and fastened jasmine buds in their hair with bobby pins before putting on their faux gold slippers.

The car was already waiting for them. It is usually the bride's mother who would accompany her but she only had her sisters. She knew that her mother would have loved to be there but she was with them in spirit, in the folds of her saree, in the twinkling of her anklets, in the scent of jasmines and in her heart. There was no time to miss her though. They were rushed to the temple. If they missed the good hour that the fortune teller had given them, she knew that the older guests would insist on rescheduling. As much as she liked dressing up, she didn't want to do this again so she told the driver to drive as fast as he could. Other than the occasional cow in the middle of the street, there was nothing in their way. Things always work out that way in the good hour.

Before the car could even stop, the door was yanked open and she was pulled out. She saw a blur of colours as she ran past the guests and up the stairs. She only stopped running when she was at the entrance of the wedding hall. She heard the chatter of guests who were still arriving and when she got on her toes she could see glimpses of the flowers on the walls. She ran through all the things she had to do when she was on the dais. She had seen it many times before but standing there, she seemed to forget everything.

A man in a white sarong walked past her as she waited for her cue to enter. He didn't have his shirt on and his belly ballooned and jiggled as he walked to the dais. She had assumed he would have arrived earlier to set everything up and begin the prayers but she didn't question it. He had officiated the wedding of hundreds of the women gathered in the hall. He could probably do it with his eyes closed.

His arrival made her even more nervous. It meant that soon she will have a thali tied around her neck and she will be someone's wife. Though she knew the man she was marrying, she didn't know a life outside of her house. She was only ever good at painting and cooking for her sisters. She didn't know how to live with someone who wasn't family but then again no one did before marriage and everyone else seemed to be faring well.

As the remainder of the guests bustled in, pushing past her, she closed her eyes. She called for her mother and she felt a warmth in her chest. Her mother always made her feel safe and today she made the bride feel calm. As she walked in with her sisters, with her mother in her mind, and sat at the dais, she felt like everything was right. The doubts she usually harboured were gone and she knew that it was because this was how it was meant to be. She believed in the universe and today it had no warnings for her. The sun was bright and flowers bloomed. It was a great day to get married.

It all went according to plan. She was married during the good hour and arrived at her new home hours later. Her husband went to take a nap the moment they got home and she got her saree off with the help of her sisters. She had to start getting ready for their wedding reception right away. She had one of her mother's sarees ready for her. When she was younger she had seen photos of her mother wearing it on her wedding day and she had asked her mother if she could have it. It was one of the only things from her mother that wasn't thrown away or incinerated when her mother was cremated. She also put on the matching bangles and earrings. It wasn't as heavy as the ones from that morning. She looked in her mirror and there on her neck was the one thing that told her that things will never be the same again. She was a wife now.

She waited in the hall for her husband to wake up and get dressed. She knew that men didn't take long to get dressed. Her father only needed fifteen minutes to get ready. She assumed her husband would be the same. Half an hour before they were scheduled to leave she went to their bedroom. She called his name and pulled his blanket off of him. That always worked on her but he didn't move. She shook him and started yelling his name but nothing happened. His eyes stayed closed. They never opened again.

She sat beside him and took his hand. The henna on her palms matched the colour of his wedding clothes. She hadn't noticed that earlier. She looked at his face and noticed a razor cut on his upper lip. It must have happened that morning. He had a scar on his forehead and she wondered where he had gotten it. His hands were soft, unlike her father's calloused ones. She guessed that it was because he didn't use his hands much at his engineering job. She didn't even know what he did there. She didn't know a lot about him. She only knew that for a few hours, she was his wife.

When the car came to pick them up, she walked out and told the driver that she needed help. He came in and she helped him carry her husband into the car. He took them to a hospital. The doctor couldn't do anything for him. She knew that but she had hope that maybe he could. She sat outside as she waited for someone to tell her what her heart already knew. She didn't have to wait long. They said he had a heart attack.

She asked someone for a phone and called her house but no one answered. Remembering the wedding reception, she called her sister's phone. When she picked up, she said, 'He's gone.'

'What do you mean? Did he run?' her sister said.

'He is d-dead,' she said. There was silence on the line.

'What happened?'

'It was a heart attack. I am at the hospital now.' She heard more voices on the other end and she heard the moment his mother found out. After telling her sister which hospital she was at, she hung up. She walked out of the hospital and got in the car. She told the driver to take her home.

She looked down at her henna hands wondering where it went wrong. She was on time for her wedding. She had kept the henna on longer than anyone else ever did. The henna stains hadn't even begun to fade yet her marriage was over. It didn't make any sense. The henna was still there. Even the ones on her feet were as vibrant as they were yesterday.

She examined each arc and curve of the spirals on her hands and feet, trying to figure out what went wrong. She didn't even realise when the car stopped until the driver cleared his throat. She looked out the window and saw the house that she had entered for the first time that morning. It wasn't the 'home' she meant when she told the driver but he was right. It was her home now. She went in and started to pack his things. She remembered her father doing it the day her mother had died.

Her husband didn't have many clothes. He had about a dozen shirts and a pair of slacks. He had shorts and faded t-shirts all stuffed in the same drawer as his underwear. She chose a shirt and took one of the pants for him to be buried in before packing them all in a garbage bag and putting it outside. Then she unpacked her suitcase. She hung up her new sarees that she had bought because her relatives had told her that her husband might want her to wear sarees. She wondered if he would have liked her better in her dresses or in a saree. It took a long time for her to unpack. The sun had set and she was still hanging up sarees.

It was late in the evening when there was a knock at her door. She opened it and her sisters threw their arms around her. They asked her how she was feeling but she didn't know how to answer them because she felt nothing but confusion. They told her that his family will handle it all.

She entertained her sisters' effort to comfort her but nothing they said reached her. She ran through the events of the day in her mind, trying to figure out what she had done wrong. The universe only punished people when they didn't follow tradition. She had protection against dark magic, so she eliminated the possibility that someone had cursed her. Long after her sisters left, she sat and pondered.

The only thing she did other than think was paint. She had painted non-stop for days after her mother had died. It had kept her busy then and now it was more helpful than ever. She painted her wedding clothes and the flowers that hung from the ceiling in the wedding hall. She painted her husband's face. It wasn't very accurate, as she didn't really remember his face. She had only seen his face twice after all. She mostly painted the henna patterns that adorned her hands and feet. Her hands grew steadier and the patterns became more refined.

She painted till there was no paint left and she was forced to leave her house to get more. She didn't have any of her usual clothes so she put on one of the new sarees and decided to walk to the marketplace instead of calling for the driver. On the way to the market, she walked by people she knew. She waved at them but they quickly turned away. She could hear whispers as she walked by. Putting it down to paranoia, she continued on.

When she reached the marketplace, she headed to her usual art stall. The woman there, a close friend of her mother's, greeted her and asked her what she would like. She was polite but something was different. She would usually make small talk and make a short shopping trip last an hour. This time though she packed the paints and canvases hurriedly and handed them to the new widow. None of the other shopkeepers spoke to her either. They handed her what she wanted and some even took extra care not to touch her.

She saw some of the women glare at her hands and she saw that the henna had not begun to fade even though they were drawn on a week ago. She pulled her saree pallu tighter around her and hid her hands as she walked home. She expected pity and sympathy from her neighbours like when her mother had died but there was only hostility. When she went to the market to sell her paintings, the woman at the art stall looked almost angry that she was there. To make matters worse, no one bought her paintings anymore.

She didn't need the money as her husband's was now hers but she felt validated when anyone bought her art because it meant that she was good at something. She had to drop out of school to help raise her sisters after her mother had passed on so she didn't have an education like they did. She only had painting.

She went to the market every day to see if anyone would buy a painting but they all just stopped by the stall and hurried off after speaking to the woman manning the stall. It was a weird sight so she decided to investigate. She hid behind the stall and listened to what the woman told her customers.

'Her husband died after the wedding. She is bad luck. You don't want this in your house,' she said.

'I heard she did it for the money. She is living there alone now using up all the money,' a customer said. 'She came here with an expensive saree. She must be celebrating. Probably looking for another man already,' the woman said.

The longer she listened the harder it got for her to breathe. She didn't think anyone would blame her for his death but then she remembered how things were with her family. She remembered how when her aunt's husband had died, they all gossiped and said that she should have looked after him better. They stopped inviting her to family gatherings because they said she brought bad luck. Some of the older women stopped their daughters from speaking to her because they were afraid that she would pass her curse on to them. She eventually left town and no one heard from her again. The people's treatment of her aunt seemed justified at that time but now that she was in her place, the young widow realised that her aunt was as innocent as she was.

To stop the gossiping from getting worse, she stopped wearing her grand sarees. She went back home to her house where her sisters now lived to borrow clothes from them but when she arrived, no one came to the door to greet her. When she tried to go inside using her key, the servants stopped her. She hammered at the door until one of her sisters was forced to see her.

'What do you want?' her sister said.

'I came to visit,' she said.

'I don't think you should come here anymore,' her sister said.

'Why not?' she asked her sister.

'The people at the temple said you will ruin our chance

of finding a husband,' her sister replied.

Her sister slammed the door in her face before she could say more. She knew how superstitious her sisters were—she was too—but she didn't think that it would apply to her. She should have known because her mother didn't hesitate to disown her aunt. Now, history repeated itself. Even the sisters that she had raised didn't want to see her.

She walked home and scrubbed at her hands and feet to remove the henna. It disappeared but left a slight reddish-brown stain. *At least now they will stop talking about me trying to find a husband*, she thought. She wore her dullest sarees as she left her house, refusing to use the driver as it would only give people more to talk about. Nothing changed though. She was the young widow who killed her husband and was now enjoying his wealth.

Her in-laws were the same. At first they tried to comfort her but as the days went on, she noticed how her mother-in-law glared at her and how her visits were scarce until she stopped visiting altogether. No one from her husband's family would talk to her but she had overheard the neighbours saying how her new family was spreading gossip about how she had killed him. There was nothing she could do to defend herself. Nothing she could say would change their minds. She was alone now and she had to get used to that.

She kept to her routine of painting, buying groceries and hurrying home for almost a year. She observed the mourning period and said her prayers, wishing that it was her who had died instead. At least then she would be missed. Instead, she was just despised and looked upon with disgust. She couldn't escape the stares and whispers even though time had forgotten about what had transpired.

One day about fifteen months after her husband's death, as she was painting, there was a knock at the front door. Hoping that it was her sisters, she rushed to the door. When she opened it, she saw someone who looked a lot like her mother.

'How are you?' the woman asked. Hearing her mother's voice, she began to cry. The woman embraced her and the girl clung on. She cried for hours but the woman didn't seem to mind. She listened as the girl told her what had happened.

'I knew that they would do that,' the woman said.

'How?'

'Because they did the same to me,' the woman said and suddenly the girl realised who it was.

'Aunty Prisha?' she said and the woman nodded. The last time she had seen her aunt, her mother had slapped the woman and told her to never come to their home again. Would her mother have done the same to her if she was alive? As much as she wanted to believe otherwise, she knew that her mother wouldn't have hesitated to kick her out.

She invited her aunt inside and as she made a cup of tea, she asked her aunt about her life after she left the village.

'I sold my wedding jewellery and bought a plane ticket. I worked in Paris at a bakery, and then I bought another plane ticket and worked in a small bar in Switzerland. I met someone in Austria and got married again. He hasn't died yet,' her aunt joked.

'Why are you here?' the girl asked.

'I heard what happened. I wanted to help you. I knew they would kick you out of the family. I knew that the people in this stupid village would act like they are better than you and blame you for what happened. I was older than you when it happened. I don't want you to waste your youth here.'

'Where would I go?' she asked.

'Anywhere you want. You have money and no one to hold you back,' she said.

Her aunt looked around the room at all the paintings and smiled.

'No one paints like you do. Why don't you go to art school?'

The thought of school had never crossed her mind. She had given up on being an artist the day her mother died. Now though, her aunt was right. There was nothing holding her back.

With the help of her aunt, she put together a portfolio of all her works. They brought tears to her aunt's eyes and it was only a surprise to the artist that she got in. She sold her jewellery, bought a plane ticket and packed her bags. She left the village that no longer loved her and never looked back.

The people say she ran away and died but those who have seen her art will recognise it in the halls of the most prestigious art museums. She now paints in the comfort of her new home where she is just a few blocks away from her aunt. She has painted many things from her past but her best-selling motifs are the ones she once wore on her hands and feet the day her husband died.

THE STORY OF SHE

~

Her funeral was as beautiful as she was. That's what we're all supposed to say, isn't it? The truth is I have never seen an uglier day. I know she has though. It is such a pity that someone so beautiful lived such an ugly life. Still, there were instances of beauty. For her, that beauty was him. We didn't see what she saw. He was ugly and that's what she became.

They met in high school when she was sixteen. He was a year older. She was always adventurous and she met him at a time when she had just begun exploring. He was the quiet kid, slow to compliment her and that set him apart from the other boys who told her she was pretty. She liked that about him because compliments mean so much more when they are scarce.

Though she liked his calming presence that was in contrast to her own, she also loved the attention the world gave her. She loved being loved and admired like any girl her age would. She ran wild down paths that opened up more paths. There was always more to see and she wanted to satiate her curiosity of everything but he didn't like that. She brought danger into his life. He feared the unknown and she wandered freely into the fog. He was content where he was and never wandered beyond the creaking metal fences of his house while she broke down fences to be free.

She tried to convince him to join her but he never did. At seventeen, jealousy took root in his heart as she explored the world. He saw how the world looked at her and he saw how her eyes lit up as she took it all in. Everyone told her it was a mistake to start something at sixteen but part of her beauty was her stubbornness and so she didn't listen. It was a mistake because he took up so much space that there was no room to explore anything else. He made her choose between him and adventure. She chose him.

She built a fantasy in her head of all the things she could do with him beside her. It used to be her dreams but he convinced her that he should be a part of them. He promised her forever and told her that all she needed was him. She gave up her friends for him because he convinced her that they were a bad influence. He told her that they would lead her astray and that she would ruin her reputation. He told her things that made her doubt herself, but she held on to adventure and to her curiosity because she wanted to feel freedom. Freedom was hard to reach because she was clinging on to her captor.

Her only mistake was that she didn't let her adventurous spirit die like he wanted it to. She tried to live her life as she wanted. He was there every step of the way blocking her path and forcing her to turn around. Sometimes she let him because she believed it was love. Someone should have told her that love does not constrict but I don't think she would have listened because she had already fallen for his snake eyes. She let him choke her and she smiled as he did.

The times when she went against his wishes were terrifying. The quiet boy found words so excruciating that it would reach her heart and rip it open. She would bleed but she patched herself up. The sad thing is he made her think that it was her fault. He told her that it wasn't in his nature to be mean. She believed him every time. What she didn't realise was that though it may not have been in his nature before, it definitely became a part of him. He broke her with words and she found ways to forgive him by blaming herself. He never apologised because she didn't think he needed to. He made her believe that she was the problem.

Their relationship consisted of a cycle of fights and forgiveness. He accused her of cheating on him whenever she wasn't available to speak to him and she had to convince him that she belonged to him. She had to answer to him about everything she ever did. She couldn't leave her house without asking for his permission. She knew that if she tried, it would only lead to a fight. It led to a fight even when she did ask because he found a way to make things sour. He made her despise the places she used to love and he made her feel that he was the only place for her. He called her the ugliest things and she believed him. The more she believed him, the uglier she got. She begged for forgiveness and he forgave her after every fight. With each fight, she let go of tiny shreds of freedom. She let go of what made her beautiful.

Everyone told her to leave him after their tenth fight in the span of a month in their first year but she carried on with him for a hundred more months and thousands of fights. Those around her could see that she was miserable yet she somehow managed to convince herself that she was happy. She told everyone that he understood her better than anyone else. They agreed because she was right. He did understand her. He understood her enough to know how to control her and break her. There was no love there. I don't think there ever was.

Sadly, she saw love where there was none. She convinced herself that the reason he behaved the way he did was because he loved her too much. She convinced herself that he was only mean because he wanted her to be better. She convinced herself that she made him that way and so she should stay because she broke him. She told herself so many lies to justify staying. She refused to see him for what he was, an insecure boy who was trying to hold on to something that didn't belong to him. She clung on tighter because she was afraid that she had wasted all those months on someone that may not have been right for her. She didn't want to start again. She was afraid that she will never find someone who understood her like he did.

There were many who could have understood her like she wanted them to. There could have been many that would have broken her heart. There could have been one that learned her favourite flower and who brought one for her each time they met and there could have been one who cared. There could have been someone who loved her for her and one who didn't have a jealous heart. There were many possibilities for happiness that she refused to explore. Instead she settled for a tempest that thrived on control. There was no adventure or curiosity that spurred her on anymore. She lived and learned about anything she could, anything that wouldn't displease him.

They got married after approximately five years. She chose him because there were no other options. She had to choose him because he didn't give her a choice. They were together long enough and it was time. No one was happy with their match except for the both of them. She was happy because she thought that marriage meant that he loved her enough to choose her while he was happy because now he owned her in name too. He was relieved because he didn't have to worry about other boys anymore.

She, on the other hand, had one boy to worry about, a boy that never became a man in all the years that she knew him. She loved that boy and that blinded her to the fact that she had become a woman while he was just that same quiet, insecure boy. It was that familiarity, that reminder that some things don't change, that she loved, so it didn't affect her. She didn't know that nothing stays the same, that sometimes bad gets worse instead of better. She learned that the hard way.

The more she acted like a woman the less he liked her. In fact, he had begun to despise her a long while ago around their twentieth fight. He stayed out of spite. He wanted to change her so he forced her to become the girl she once was. He graduated from harsh words to light taps on her cheek, which then escalated to slaps. He had her beg for forgiveness like she used to do, except now she apologised for his hand hurting when he punched her. He told her that she was the problem. He didn't need to convince her because she had already convinced herself. She made excuses for his behaviour saying, 'That's not him' and 'You don't know him like I do'. The excuse she used the most was, 'He's not usually like this' accompanied with 'It's my fault'.

She strung a long string of excuses and that string led her to her grave. He had hit her too hard one day and she had bled to death. In reality, I think she died long before she breathed her last. I hope that in her final moments she found clarity. I hope she gave herself a chance to hate him. I hope that she at least didn't blame herself. As they laid her in her coffin, no one recognised her. He had marred her and destroyed every ounce of beauty she had. She was as ugly as her life was and no amount of makeup they put on her corpse could change that.

Her story wasn't a happy one. The only consolation is that it wasn't a long one. It isn't fair to call it her story because it is filled with him. The story of she should have been about her, about how she lived and laughed and died of old age with her loved ones there to tell her how much they loved her but she wrote this story and she wrote her end. The story of her is the story of him.

FISHES AND PROMISES

She frequented the port every morning to watch the boats come in. There was one boat in particular that she waited for. As she spotted the yellow cedar wood of his boat slowly making its way to the dock, she checked her reflection in the water. Her hair was unruly because of the wind but she hoped that he would find it lovely. He found a lot of things lovely: the sunset, the ever-shifting colour of fish scales in peak sunlight, and today, her dandelion coloured dress. He spotted her as he docked his boat and he watched as she ran to him. Yes, today, she was the loveliest thing he saw.

As she got closer to the end of the dock, the aroma of fresh fish permeated her senses. It is a smell she found herself looking forward to. She hopped onto his boat, almost throwing him off, but he was used to it so he braced himself.

'You're late,' she said, as she tried to pick up the net that held hundreds of fishes. He helped her with the net and together they threw it onto the already stained dock. He set up his table and she helped him arrange the fish in rows. As they waited for the usual wave of customers, he told her about his trip. She sat on one of the crates with folded legs and listened to him, wishing she could have gone too. She didn't know that he would have liked nothing more.

When the customers arrived, she watched him use the back of his knife to remove the fish scales before he chopped each fish into small pieces. He left some whole for those who request it. She stayed long after the customers were gone, her dress stained with fish guts and her heart filled with him. She walked home with a fish wrapped in brown paper that her mother had told her to pick up hours before. Her mother yelled because lunch would be late but she didn't hear her because she was lost in thoughts of him. Love found her in a flea market on a dock in the scorching sun. In her diary I found an entry that read:

Though the world was a fishy mess
It meant the world that he loved my dress.
He fulfills my every wish
Though it always seems to smell like fish.

He took her hand one day after all the fish were sold and she didn't mind that his hand was slimy and sticky and covered in fish blood, staining her own. He smelled putrid but she didn't mind that either because she liked being with him. They sat on the dock, legs swinging beneath them, just inches away from the water. In the dimming sunlight they looked out at the sea and spoke about what lay beyond. She told him that someday she would like to see the world and that she hoped he would be there with her. They walked along the shoreline and made footprints in the sand. The tide washed them away but for just a second, they left their mark on the world. That day he gave her his heart and it meant a lot to a girl who had nothing, for now she had something to call her own. When she got home that day, she wrote:

I never quite enjoyed the sand
But I forgot that when he took my hand.
He gave me something I've never known
With him I feel a little less alone.

All night she thought about him and she never left his thoughts. He thought about her eyes, her smile, her heart and she dreamt of something she decided to call love. They couldn't wait till morning, till they could see each other again. They met at the dock every day and spoke till sunset. Though they spoke for hours there was always more to say. The boy who used to speak to fish now shared his dreams with the quiet girl who he first saw sketching on the dock as her hair billowed in the wind. He found her lovely then but now he was slowly beginning to realise that she might be his everything. She felt the same about him. She wrote:

I used to dream of reaching the sea line
And seeing a world I could call mine
From the first moment I saw you
I made you part of that dream too.
I would like to have you beside me
To navigate this world and be free
For there is something beyond the horizon
I think there lies our salvation.

She snuck out one day before the sun could rise, the shadow of the fading moon in sight. She saw him on the dock with his net and his boat, ready to greet the sea.

'You forgot something,' she told him and he smiled and offered her his hand. She was nervous as she stepped onto the boat. Though she loved the sea, she hadn't gone past the docks. But when she took his hand she wasn't nervous anymore. In his boat made of yellow cedar they met the sun. He taught her how to steer the boat and told her about the wind. She asked him about mermaids, whales, dolphins, and squids. He told her one of those things doesn't exist but she insisted that whales were real. By the time the fish woke up, she knew more than she ever did. He taught her how to cast a net and when they pulled in the catch, she threw her arms around him. He had learned something that day too. He learned that he loved her more than he ever thought he could.

As they arranged the fish on the table to sell, he found an oyster amongst the fish. Though he knew that the chances of finding a pearl were one in ten thousand, he believed that they were lucky. They found each other out of seven billion people after all. He was right. There, snuggled in the mollusc, was a beautiful pearl. He gave her the pearl as a promise of forever. She told him she would hold him to that. In her diary she wrote:

Today we found something precious
We also found a pearl.

They had many adventures together. They camped out on the beach and cooked crabs along the shore. They mapped out stars and had treasure hunts. They even built a boat from a chestnut tree they chopped down together. He painted their names on the side. He told her they would leave on this boat someday.

For a while the sea was their friend and their young lives were filled with fish of every season. But the seas are unpredictable and nothing capable of destruction and chaos makes for a good friend. She waited at the docks for him one day almost a year to the day they first met, but he didn't show up. She sat at the docks for hours, long past sunset and into twilight but there was no sign of his yellow cedar boat. She came back every day and waited, though the other women mourned their loved ones. Surely she would've felt him die. Surely he wouldn't break his promise. She held on to the pearl he had given her. She refused to mourn.

Months passed and no boats came in. The women began to look for other means of sustenance and income. One by one they stopped visiting the docks. The sea that once brought them delight was now their enemy. No one fished and the crabs took over the beach. Though the others left, she kept her eyes trained on the horizon, hoping that someday he would come back.

You promised me forever
But I can't have that without you
You promised you and me
Did you leave me for the sea?

She waited till waiting wasn't an option anymore. It wasn't in her to just sit and wait. She didn't believe he would leave her, so she decided to look for him. She could feel that he was alive. She trusted that feeling. After months of avoiding his cabin, she opened the door. Around her were memories of them. She collected each trinket and piled them into a burlap sack. She knew what she had to do. She went to where he had stored their chestnut boat and though she was afraid of the sea without him, she was determined. She visited all the places they had been one last time and collected supplies for a long journey. She didn't know where the sea would take her but she knew it wouldn't lead her home again.

She said goodbye to her mother who gave her blessings for the journey ahead. Her mother knew before she did that she would go someday. Keeping in mind everything he taught her, she set off, hopping off the dock onto a boat that had never faced the sea. She looked to the stars and the direction of the wind as she charted her way to the horizon. All the while she kept the pearl he had given her close to her heart. She heard his voice tell her what to do and she followed.

She steered further out into the sea and turned around. Her old life was gone. The dock was no longer in sight. She had reached the horizon and she could see another in the distance. He told her they would leave on this boat someday and they did because she carried him in her heart and mind as little by little she made her way across a small body of sea. She was careful with her supplies and it took her far.

There was a lot that she didn't know about the sea but what she did know saw her through. She didn't keep count of how many sunrises went by before she found another dock. She tied her boat on a pole with a rope and stepped onto a wooden deck that smelled all too familiar. She was only there to collect supplies but something made her want to explore the village. She asked around if any boats had made their way to the village in the past few months. They told her that many boats had crashed in the storm that happened during the monsoon season and that many of the fishermen were at the doctor's house. She contained her excitement and hoped that he would be there. She had a feeling that he was. She followed the instructions they gave her and it led her to a longhouse made of timber.

She climbed up a ladder leading to the entrance and found rows of beds facing each other. Someone asked her who she was looking for and she told them his name as her heart hammered in her chest. *He has to be here,* she thought. Her heart told her he was and it was right. She yelled his name as she ran through the longhouse. He had dreamt of her for months and believed that he was hearing her in his dreams. He realised he was wrong when he sat up in his bed and saw her run to him. He had fractured his leg when his boat had crashed into the dock but he stood up when he saw her and limped to her. She closed the distance between them and after being strong for months, she cried. They both did.

She helped him to his bed and he asked her how she found him. It was easy for him to believe that she made her way to him because he knew her. She told him that the sea was a small distance to travel because she was only thinking of him. He told her he loved her for the first time and she told him she felt the same. They fished and reminisced as his leg healed and not long after that they began to make a life for themselves in the new village. He gave her the forever he promised and they were never apart again.

She didn't have many diary entries about her life with him. I think it's because she was too busy living to linger on memories. The last thing she wrote was on the day before she died. It reads:

In fish guts and slimy hands
I have loved you
In stained docks and stinking ships
I have loved you

In sandy beaches and rising tides,
I have loved you
In pearls in oysters and chestnut trees
I have loved you
We reach another horizon that I will cross before you
I leave you with I love you.

I don't know if he had a chance to read her words because he followed her just hours later. His last words were that he couldn't let her wait long because he had promised her forever. He kept his promise and sailed away with her.

THE TRAGEDY OF TORTOISE SHELLS

I once watched a troop of tortoises saunter in the sweltering sun. The only thing that surrounded them was a large expanse of nothing and planes of jagged rock. As they meandered, their calloused feet, which resemble stumps, left indents in the sand. They kicked up a sandstorm with each step they took and left dust in their wake. The crunch of sand created a melody that echoed in the nothingness. In spite of the sandstorm, the motif on their mosaic shells seemed almost golden in the sun. It was a serene sight, watching giants plough the land.

There is an Indian superstition that every good thing is followed by something bad. It is why they warn against laughing too much. They say it invites tears. It's something I have been told ever since I was young. Coincidence or fate, I don't know which one it was, but the serene sight turned into a nightmare in a matter of moments. One of the tortoises left the safety of the sand and wandered onto the rocks that formed a steep plane. It reached the edge of the rock and as its elongated neck stretched out to take in the sky, it lost its balance and tipped over the edge. I assumed that it died but it was very much worse.

The tortoise had landed on its back. It struggled to get up but the only thing it managed to do was resemble an erratic see-saw. I don't know how long it struggled. Its movements slowed after a while and I could sense it giving up. I was told that it was suffocating as it lay there in the scorching sun. It reminded me of Humpty Dumpty, how he fell off a wall and broke. I think the tortoise would have preferred that fate even if there was no one to put him back together again because the hours of suffering it went through must have been excruciating. Did it regret reaching for the sun as it boiled to death in the sand? As it died I thought of how the only sanctuary it had ever known was the one that let it down.

I watched as its eyes bled out from being fried alive and I was reminded of the day that they found her.

Her tortoise shell was a hull that overflowed with delight and displeasure. There was curiosity and caution, pleasure and pain. It was a pretty shell and that was all that mattered to those around her. Rarely if ever did she find someone who cared about anything other than the twirls and spirals of her shell. They didn't care about how her mind was a time bomb that went off in explosive silence and how to hide the pain she dug her nails into her skin. They didn't notice the dried blood in her fingernails or the way that she seemed to be filled with nothing but anxiety. Her days were filled with thoughts of death and they followed her into her dreams. She needed help but she never asked for it for fear that they would see her broken shell for what it was. I would love to tell you that she found someone who looked beyond her shell but this is not that kind of story. In this story she found someone in the sandstorm and called him hers.

He was nothing like her. He never second-guessed himself. He was funny without being self-deprecating. He looked for silver linings where she only saw nimbostratus clouds. He was the careless to her caution and he made her laugh. In short, the hull of his shell contrasted her own and she liked that.

She liked it because she liked herself better when she was with him. She swallowed who she was so that he would find her as interesting as she found him. When she was with him she made sure that he never saw the darkness that she harboured. Each moment with him was spent ensuring that he fell in love with her. She didn't care that it wasn't her that he loved. She wasn't sure how she felt about him but she liked how he liked her. She changed the motifs on her shell for him and he fell for the pretty colours. It wasn't surprising to her because she was used to playing a part. She played a functional human being every day after all.

She played her part so well that eventually they got married. He liked having someone who was carefree just like him. He liked that they shared the same interests and how she understood him. He fell in love with himself and didn't realise it.

On her end, she was happy that she got what she wanted. He helped her keep her dark thoughts at bay because she filled her thoughts with him. Each time an anxious thought let itself in, like thoughts of what the world would be like without him, she buried it by asking him to tell her a story. He was her distraction and all she had to do to keep him was be there for him. It didn't seem like that much of a sacrifice to swallow her pain to be someone he loved.

The thing about having a soul that is ripping is that the seam continues to rip even when you ignore it. The hull of her shell brimmed with everything she didn't want him to see. Every time something threatened to show, she dragged it back down. She clasped her hands together to keep them from trembling and when her hands were cold she made sure he didn't take her hand. She kept her shell pristine for him so that he wouldn't leave. She was intent on preserving his happiness and the happiness that she had manufactured for herself.

The day she made him the happiest was the day she gave him a daughter. He looked at the little girl covered in tendrils of blood mixed with a glutinous chartreuse yellow like it was the most beautiful thing he had ever seen. In contrast, exhausted beyond belief, she looked down at her daughter and instead of happiness, she felt repugnance and revulsion. It was ugly. It looked wrong, like it didn't belong. She didn't like how it felt in her arms. It wriggled and gurgled. Its cries overwhelmed her senses and made her want to scream. She wanted it far away from her. She wanted to throw it out the window. The moment those thoughts entered her mind she pushed them down. She knew that that was not how a mother was supposed to react to her child. She told herself that it was the blood she was repulsed by. It wasn't.

Her feelings didn't disappear even after the baby was clean. It was placed in a cradle next to her bed and she turned away from it right away though she was still in pain. She could hear the little sounds it made, hiccups and gurgling. It made her want to scratch at her ears. She swallowed the urge by digging her fingernails into her skin. It distracted her from the noise. The thing that repulsed her most was feeding it. When the nurse handed her the baby she didn't know what to do. She couldn't imagine holding it so close to her and letting it suckle on her. She wanted to tell them to take it away. Instead, she played her part. She fought the urge to pull it off her right breast as it clung on, greedily sucking and tugging, asking her for more. It always wanted more. She could feel its gums against her skin and as someone who hated being touched, she felt violated by its presence. She looked down at its greedy little face and all she wanted was to get as far away from it as she could. She thought going home would change how she felt about her child. It didn't.

She unlocked the front door of her house and she felt happy for a moment. This was her space. She could smell remnants of her vanilla-scented candle in the air. It never seemed to fade. The familiar creak of the wooden floorboards comforted her as she walked through the house, taking in the feeling of home. It made her think that perhaps it was the atmosphere and stress of the hospital that was affecting her. Now that she was in her own space, it will all go back to normal, she thought. As her husband brought the baby in, laughing as he spoke to the thing, the sliver of happiness turned to a flare of anger. The thing was in her space. She rushed to her room as fast as she could and locked herself in the bathroom.

In the bathroom, she took deep breaths and told herself that she could do this. The nurses had given her a list of things to do for the child every day. *All I have to do is go down the list*, she thought. She cleared her mind, just like she used to do to get into character, and she told herself that she will love her child. It would be her greatest performance.

It was usually easy for her to pretend but this time she found herself exhausted at the attempt. It felt as if each vein in her body carried hatred for the little thing. Every time she looked at it, she felt tears form. Every time it cried she contemplated ignoring it or smothering it. She did neither. She clung on to the list and checked whether it was hungry or if it soiled itself. She played with the child when her husband was around, gritting her teeth as she did. When she was forced to comfort the child when it cried, she took long hot showers to burn off the feeling of its skin against hers. She did everything she could to carry on the act.

The first test of her fortitude came in the form of ordure. She had pushed through all the hurdles the day presented her and she had sat down for a cup of tea. That's when the usual wailing began. Though she was used to the sound at that point, she still hated it. She knew it had to be time to clean it, as she had already fed it. She undid the pins of the linen cloth that swaddled it and the putrid smell she had gotten used to wafted to her. A mustard yellow explosion greeted her. Earlier that day it had been a sunflower yellow and in the afternoon it had been rather green. She pulled out the wet wipes and got to work.

As she wiped away the excrement, she kept her mind on mundane things like what to cook for dinner and her grocery list. She was so distracted by her thoughts that she accidentally picked up a wad of mustard yellow. The moment she felt the warm liquid on her fingers, she froze. A million things ran through her mind. She knew she needed to get clean. She knew she had to get to the bathroom. She knew she needed to finish cleaning the thing. She knew exactly what to do. The only problem was that she couldn't move her feet.

She felt her eyes start to sting and as everything around her became a blur, she let her tears fall. The longer she stood there staring down at her yellow fingers, the more the tears fell. She cried until the only coherent thought she could muster was that she needed to get rid of her fingers. *It's such an obvious solution*, she thought. She walked to the kitchen and as she picked up a chopper she heard the doorbell ring. She glanced at the clock and saw that it was the usual time her husband got home. *I can't let him see me like this*, she thought. She quickly got cleaned and rushed to the baby. Her husband greeted her as she cleaned it and joked about the smell. She had managed to keep up the act another day.

She was faced with tests every day. Some days she didn't want to get out of bed to comfort the crying child. On the days her breasts were dry and chapped at the nipples she wanted to refuse to feed it. She cried more than she ever did and she lost track of days and nights as she began to live in her head. As the days went on there was a ringing in her head that wouldn't go away. Her only respite from it was sleep but she couldn't seem to get any. The moment she laid down, she would hear crying. She would get up to check on the child but would find it fast asleep. There were times when she would wake her husband up to check on it but he would tell her that he heard nothing. To prevent herself from disturbing his sleep, she wandered the corridor outside their bedroom till she fell asleep from exhaustion. Still, the ringing in her head remained. In her dreams the baby ate at her remains as she lay there on her bed trying to get away. She couldn't escape the crying either. It only got louder as everything around her faded. She was just a tortoise on her back, boiling in the sun, flailing and struggling with no one to help.

The only thing she held on to was preserving her shell.

It never mattered what was happening on the inside before so why should it matter now, she thought. She carried on with her daily life as she always did: meeting her neighbours, keeping the house clean, being there for her husband, and making sure that no one suspected anything was wrong. To her, nothing was wrong. It had always been this way for her. It was just a little worse now because she was split in two, one half ready to saw the baby in two and the other intent on playing her part. She wanted the thing to hurt like it was hurting her but she knew that if she gave in to it, the play would end and people would see. She couldn't have that. She had faith in herself that she would be able to pull it off.

Just like the tortoise suffocated as its shell let it down, so did she slowly deteriorate mentally under the weight of her thoughts. No one realised she was suffocating. Her shell was shined and primed. No one could see the growing cracks. The thing that broke this tortoise's back was a family trip to the seaside. It was a change she wasn't prepared for. She didn't know what part to play as her husband entertained the child so she did what she always did when she was unsure. She went for a walk. She left the child with her husband and wandered to the highest peak. Perhaps she was reaching for the sun when she fell. Perhaps she was looking for the peace she once knew and reached out to grab it. Whatever she was reaching for I hope she found it even if it was for just a moment.

When they found her, she was long gone. She had bled to death. I don't think she fought to stay alive like the tortoise did. I don't think she struggled. I don't think she called for help. I think she gave up the moment she hit the ground. I think she gave in to her mind and let go of the pain that had plagued her for as long as she could remember. That was her curtain call. Alas, there was no applause.

EXISTENCE PRECEDES ESSENCE

Aristotle and Plato believed that we are all born with a purpose, an essence. For these philosophers our essence or purpose precedes our existence or our birth. They believed that in order to live a good life, one must adhere to one's essence. The notion of free will is then simmered down to making choices based on an innate need to learn one's purpose and ultimately fulfill it.

Existentialist Jean-Paul Sartre, though, disagreed. He believed that we are not born with a purpose. Rather, we find our purpose as we learn and grow. For him, our existence precedes our essence. We are born a blank slate and the choices we make determine our purpose. We are imbued with freedom and it is only in utilising our freedom by making choices free of outside influences that we live authentically.

I, like many before me and certainly after me, am not afforded the same freedom. We are limited in our choices. When we are born we are given a purpose and our job is to live up to it or perish. In the realm of limited choices, I have no choice but to formulate my own. Every day I do something that opens a door that wasn't there before. Sometimes I do nothing at all. That too is a choice, an authentic one because it was made by me.

My week starts with a trip to the marketplace. I head to the seafood stall and I see that it is not crowded yet. There is only a middle-aged woman with a walking stick standing by the fish. I hear her haggle with the grocer. She is a master of her craft and I know the grocer stands no chance against her. She points out how the gills of the fish are grey and how the eyes are dull. I can't tell the difference between any of the fish's eyes because they are dead but she points out the varying degrees of yellowing sclera easily. She pokes at the fish's stomach and tells the grocer that she can feel its guts coming loose. Other customers begin to gather and it doesn't take long for the grocer to wrap her fish up in newspaper and practically throw it at her.

She unzips her faded handbag to pay the grocer and I see her stiffen. She digs through her bag, creating a small tornado of receipts but there is no cash in sight. She contemplates leaving the fish but decides against it. Then I see her watch the grocer and I know she wants to ask him if she can pay another day. I don't think she will succeed after her haggling and after a while I see that she realises that too. I watch as she tries to tuck the fish away in her billowing skirt but she doesn't have pockets. Her bag is too small to fit the fish and the crowd is dissipating so there is no way she would get away with stealing it.

'Good morning, Aunty,' I say and she turns to me. She mumbles a good morning.

I choose my fish based on what the woman had said and when it is time to pay I tell the grocer, 'I will pay for her too.'

The woman looks shocked and begins to thank me. I tell her that it is no problem. She tells me that she will pay me back but I tell her that it is not necessary. She asks me who I am and I tell her my name. I spend the rest of the shopping trip with her as she continues to ask me questions about myself. She teaches me how to choose the best tomatoes and hits the watermelons to see which one is the juiciest. When I tell her goodbye, she thanks me again. I head home and give the fish to my mother. She compliments me on my choice of fish.

The next day I leave early for the temple. I put on my best Punjabi suit and walk down a street overrun with potholes. Nothing is too far to reach by foot in this town. The furthest places can be reached by bus. Avoiding reckless motorcyclists, I reach the temple ten minutes later. I take off my slippers and wash my feet at the taps that line the outer walls of the temple before stepping onto holy ground. I make a stop at each statue and pray for blessings. When I am done, as I am leaving, someone calls my name.

'What are the chances of us meeting again?' the woman from the marketplace says.

'I come here every morning,' I tell her.

'Are you leaving?' she asks and I nod.

She asks me to join her and though I am starving, I follow her as she makes her rounds. I help her where I can and I feel her eyes on me, scrutinising my every move. Before I leave she insists on buying me some food from the stalls outside. She asks me to choose a stall and I choose the one closest to me. She tells me that that is her favourite. I tell her it is mine too. We sit on the bottom steps of the temple and eat a wada pao[1] each.

She asks me where I live and I tell her it is ten minutes away. I notice her limping as she walks and I ask her where

---

[1] A bun stuffed with a potato dumpling with chutney as a dip.

her walking stick is. She tells me that her son had taken it to work with him as she had forgotten to get it out of his car. I offer her my arm and tell her that I will walk her back. She clings on to me and half an hour later we reach her house.

She invites me inside for a cup of tea and though I needed to get home, I join her on her patio. I text my mother to tell her that I will be back late. The last time I went home late without letting her know, she had begun a search party for me. I tell the woman that and she laughs. She tells me how she never knows where her son is and how sometimes she is afraid he won't come home. I ask her why and she says I will understand when I am a mother.

She talks for about an hour about her life and I wonder how long it has been since she has had someone to talk to.

'I used to take the bus every morning to the temple. That is where I met my husband. He took the bus to work at the same time. He kept his bag on the seat and I told him to move it. After that he always kept a seat for me with his bag until I got on board,' she says.

'How long after did you get married?' I ask.

'We only knew each other for three months. The neighbours started gossiping about us and to stop them, he told his parents about us and we got engaged.'

'That's fast,' I say and she tells me that she is glad it happened the way it did because it all worked out in the end.

As we are talking a car arrives. She glances at the clock and says, 'He's early.'

She grabs my hand and says, 'Come, I will introduce you.' She pulls me to the car and the person inside opens the door.

When he gets out of the car, I have to bite my cheek to

stop from smiling. He offers me his hand and I shake it.

'Can you send her to her house? A young girl shouldn't walk home alone,' she says.

He nods and I get in the front seat. I tell her I will see her at the temple or the market and she tells me to visit any time.

On the ride home, he asks me about myself. I tell him what I told his mother. I ask him about himself and it is as if I already knew him. I had thought that his mother was exaggerating about him as mothers do but she was right. He is handsome, funny, and a little arrogant.

When he reaches my house, I thank him and as I am closing the car door he says, 'I'll see you at the temple tomorrow.' I nod and he smiles before driving off.

The next morning I am up earlier than usual. I get dressed in my best Punjabi suit and curl the bottom of my hair. I leave before my mother wakes up because she will know what I am doing right away.

As I am fastening the clasp of my sandals a car arrives. He winds down the window and his mother says, 'My son wanted to give you a lift.' He gets out of the car quickly and opens the door for me. I smile and thank him and he starts to blush.

He is quieter than he was yesterday but so am I. As his mother fills the silence, he glances at me through the rear-view mirror. Our eyes meet and I quickly look away. I see him smile and my heart starts to race.

We reach the temple in no time and he opens the door for me after helping his mother out. As we are walking, I feel his hand brush against mine and I let my hand linger for a while before quickening my pace.

'What are you praying for?' he asks as I face one of the

statues. His mother has gone to another part of the temple.

'I can't tell you that,' I say.

'Why not? Because it won't come true?' he says.

'Stop distracting her. She's praying,' his mother says out of nowhere and he jumps. He mumbles an apology as I try not to laugh.

He excuses himself and I see him walk out of the temple. I stay with his mother and finish making the rounds with her. When we are done, we head to the entrance again. There, I see him with a small paper bag filled with sweets. He offers me one and I take it. When his mother looks away, he slips me a chrysanthemum. As I am putting it in my bag, I feel someone watching and when I look up, I see him. He smiles and I turn away as my heart races again.

He helps his mother to the car and as he opens the door for me, he says, 'Do you want to know what I prayed for?' I nod and he smirks.

Instead of sending me home, his mother asks if I would mind if we head to the market right away. I tell her I don't. I wouldn't have minded anything to be honest, as long as he was there. My phone rings and I tell my mother that I am heading to the market.

'I would like to meet you mother,' his mother says.

'You can meet her when you send me home later,' I say. I can feel him looking at me through the rear-view mirror again so I keep my eyes on my lap as I talk. The trip to the market goes by quickly because I am nervous about how my mother will react. I grab anything I see and hope that my mother will know what to do with it.

I text my mother before we leave the market to say that we will have guests and she tells me she will make tea. I try to stay calm but I feel my hands get cold and my stomach feels like jelly. By the time we reach my house I am ready to hurl.

Nothing special happens when my mother meets his. We only plan when our engagement will be. You may think this all happened so fast. We only just met after all. In truth though we have known each other for three years now. We had our rings ready. We were on the same plane heading to university. We were in the same classes and the same clubs. We competed with our grades and played badminton in the evenings outside our dorms. We had our first kiss when he walked me to my dorm one night and we have shared many more kisses over the years. I love him and he loves me but the only thing that stood in our way was our families. We didn't try to convince them. We didn't even try to tell them about us. As long as we were the ones who chose our match, there would always be a problem.

That is why a few days ago when I went to the market, I went with extra cash to help a lady who would be buying fish that morning. I knew she wouldn't have money because her son would make sure to take her purse out of her bag. When I went to the temple, it was the first time in years that I had even stepped on holy ground. He told me his mother's schedule and told me to be ready. When she met me there, she was on schedule. He told me his mother's favourite things so I made sure to mention that those were my favourites too. She didn't leave her walking stick in her son's car. He put it in there so I would have a chance to walk her home. He knew his mother would insist on tea. We planned that that is where we would meet.

Now, we sit with our mothers and our intertwined hands are hidden under my scarf. We don't have to hide anymore. Soon our wedding will be arranged for us and all we have to do is say yes. I wish we didn't have to go through so much just to tell our parents we were together but if we didn't, there is no way we would have gotten here.

I would never have had the chance to marry him because my parents would never have met him. He wouldn't have been an option for me. Like I said, I, like many before me and certainly after me, am not afforded the same freedom. We are limited in our choices. When we are born we are given a purpose and our job is to live up to it or perish. In the realm of limited choices, I have no choice but to formulate my own. Every day I do something that gets me one step closer or opens a door that wasn't there before. Today I chose the man I will marry and he chose me too.

SNOW WHITE AND TAR BLACK

In the same room of the same place in the same corner of the world on the same day at the same hour in the same moment in time, two umbilical cords were cut. Two bottoms were slapped and the crying was in accord. Both families were a little disappointed that they were girls but they congratulated the new mothers when they came to visit her. Both mothers-in-law and mothers, now grandmothers took turns picking up their grandchild and pulled at the napkin covering the baby's bottom to see the colour of its buttocks. It may seem like a bizarre thing to do but they learned from their mothers that the initial colour that the baby is born with is not what it remains. Like their mothers they looked to the buttocks to check what the colour of the baby's skin will be as they grow up. And that is where the two girls born in the same room of the same place in the same corner of the world on the same day at the same hour in the same moment in time differed. The difference meant nothing and everything.

Her family didn't call her ugly but they didn't go out of their way to compliment the darker baby. They mentioned how she had her mother's lips and eyes.

'She should have taken her colour too,' they said when they were out of earshot.

They said that she looked healthy but that it was a pity

that she came out so tar-like. They averted their gaze when the child was brought out and they could barely hide their disgust when they were forced to carry the child. No one ventured near the child when they came to visit the mother which was unusual as anyone would be excited to see a newborn as adorable as her. They called her Tar Black behind the family's back and that nickname stuck.

On the other side of the coin was her twin in all but name. This baby girl was fair-skinned just like her mother. She had large dark eyes which looked at everything in wonder. She didn't like when people carried her and cried to go back to her mother. Those who saw her said that the child was the prettiest baby girl they had ever seen. They pinched her cheeks till they turned pink and marvelled at every little thing she did. Those who came to visit insisted on carrying her, though she made a fuss, and they joked about taking her home with them. When she laughed they felt their hearts melt and they tried hard to make her laugh. All those who came to visit the mother brought new clothes and expensive toys for the child. They made any excuse to visit and when they did they would stay long past the time they should leave, content with being around the child. They called her Snow White and parents took note of her for their sons someday.

On the first day of school seven years later in the same town in the same school, the two girls who were born on the same day in the same room met. They were seated next to each other and the girls, who once cried in accord, became fast friends like kids that age often do. They showed off their stationary to each other and exchanged erasers, a bow-shaped one for one shaped like a slice of cake. They told each other about how they prepared for school, what they had for breakfast, where they bought their backpacks and all about their favourite shows. They did that every day, each girl talking to her heart's content. They went home each day looking forward to school the next because they could see their new friend. They brought lunch to share and they sat together at recess, continuing their stories. When it came time to celebrate their birthdays, both brought a cake to share with the class. They loved having the same birthday. They insisted on having matching dresses and through the years they took turns having parties at each other's houses.

When the time came for high school, there was no question of being separated from one another. They went shopping for new pinafores and new shoes together and bought new bags and new stationery. They planned to tie their hair the same way and they even bought matching planners. Being as intelligent as the other, both girls were placed in the same class in the same school. Naturally, they sat next to each other. They walked to school together, meeting at the bus stop and choosing to walk instead of taking the bus so they would have more time to talk. They continued as they did when they were younger until the day came when they couldn't do that anymore.

It started with a boy. He was the neighbour of Tar Black. She used to play with him when they were young and now that they were older, she had developed a crush on him. The problem was he didn't feel the same. He had seen both girls walk home all the time and had fallen in love with the fair-skinned beauty he had heard so much about. Snow White didn't know he existed and he made it his mission to get her to notice him. Whenever she was at Tar Black's house he would make any excuse to go there. He would make the dumbest jokes and tell the most bizarre stories to them. All the things he did to get her attention only made Tar Black like him more. Tar Black told Snow White how much she liked him and Snow White told her to tell him how she felt. It was his reply that caused a small rift in their friendship.

'I really like you,' Tar Black had told him one evening when Snow White had left to go home early.

He looked surprised and being as reckless as young boys are, he said, 'I like your friend.' When she asked the boy why, she wished she hadn't. 'She is so fair and pretty,' he had said.

Tar Black had always noticed how people ignored her when Snow White was around. It was difficult to ignore how whenever Snow White spoke everyone would stop and listen. It was in contrast to how they were with her. Snow White received better grades for the same work she submitted and everyone wanted to be Snow White's friend. They complimented Snow White on the smallest things while all of Tar Black's achievements went unnoticed. Tar Black had never been jealous though she was irritated by how all Snow White had to do was smile to get anything she wanted. She was annoyed by how she had to work hard to be noticed and even then she was overshadowed by her best friend. Her love for her friend had stopped her from feeling jealous before but now she couldn't stop the bitterness in her heart from spreading. Little by little she began to despise her best friend. Snow White had stolen the one thing she wanted so Tar Black decided that she would do the same to her.

Being friends for almost ten years Tar Black knew everything about Snow White. She knew all her hopes and dreams and she knew that the one thing Snow White wanted was the scholarship awarded for best student. Tar Black began to study more than she ever did. She kept up the façade of being Snow White's friend while plotting to steal the scholarship from her. She took part in all the same sports that Snow White was in and trained hard to be better than her. The sad thing is that no matter what she did, she was always second best. She tried her hardest but she couldn't get recommendation letters from her teachers as they had all given one to Snow White. Snow White was better than her in every way and, though they were neck and neck academically, Snow White was given the scholarship. In the same room of the same place in the same corner of the world on the same day at the same hour in the same moment in time two girls who were great friends severed their bond. The day the result was announced Tar Black never spoke to Snow White again.

They went their separate ways, Snow White following her dream of becoming a teacher while Tar Black became a clerk at her father's accounting firm. Snow White only got more beautiful and everywhere she went she made friends. Her students loved her because she was as kind as she was beautiful. By the time Snow White was twenty-one years old she had already received over a dozen proposals. She got to meet the families and choose who to marry. She had the luxury of falling in love and getting married whenever she wanted.

It was different for Tar Black. She hated her life. No matter how many skin-whitening creams she used, none of them worked. Each of her job interviews went smoothly but she was never called back for final interviews. She knew it was because of her face. She had gotten the best results in university and had abundant job experience but no one wanted to hire a woman, let alone an unattractive one. As a final resort, she took the job at her father's firm. Tar Black was also unlucky in the marriage market. Her parents had to work hard to find people who were willing to make a marriage proposal. The moment they saw her though the families would apologise and leave. They wanted fair grandchildren and Tar Black could not give them that. They didn't bother hiding their disgust with the colour of her skin. They told her that they were not interested and left. No one stayed to get to know her. She was sure that if they just gave her a chance they would at least like her. Alas, just like all the other times in her life, she didn't get what she wanted.

The day came when a wedding invitation arrived at Tar Black's house. She felt her heart break as she read the name on the card. She had thought that Snow White would have gotten married long before. She had heard the news of her engagement and she was filled with jealousy. Snow White had won. She would always win. She didn't want to attend the wedding but her parents dragged her along. They told her that maybe she could meet someone there. She bought the most expensive saree she could find and went to a salon to get her makeup done. She wanted to outshine Snow White on her wedding day. Years of holding a grudge had only made her despise Snow White and she wanted Snow White to feel, just once, how she felt each time Snow White was around.

This story doesn't end well for Tar Black. She never could be better than Snow White, even at her best. No one even noticed her when Snow White walked into the room. Snow White looked more beautiful than she ever did and to add insult to injury, she had found a man who matched her beauty. He looked at her with so much love and she looked like it was the happiest day of her life. Tar Black never had that. I didn't follow her story to see what happened next for her but I did learn that years later she and Snow White found themselves in the same room of the same place in the same corner of the world on the same day at the same hour in the same moment in time, and two umbilical cords were cut. Two bottoms were slapped and the crying was in accord. Both mothers-in-law and mothers, now grandmothers took turns picking up their grandchild and pulled at the napkin covering the baby's bottom to see the colour of its buttocks. It may seem like a bizarre thing to do but they learned from their mothers that the initial colour that the baby is born with is not what it remains. Like their mothers they looked to the buttocks to check what the colour of the baby's skin would be as they grew up. And that is where the path of two girls born in the same room of the same place in the same corner of the world on the same day at the same hour in the same moment in time diverged.

COTTON CANDY CLOUDS AND GRAVEYARD STARS

I once knew a girl who found dragons in cotton candy clouds and made up stories about them in her head. I remember her story about a frog that leapt so high that his feet fell off and as the clouds shifted, she saw a fairy with slices of pizza for wings. There was a cat with a huge belly that snacked on snowflakes and dinosaurs were never extinct in her world. She built mesmerizing worlds and took me along with her as she explored broken paths and wilting dreams, creaking carousels and mountain peaks. I wanted to live in the worlds she built because she saw beauty in everything, so much so that everything she touched became beautiful, even me.

Our adventures were always perilous which suited her because she was brave. She liked to climb to the highest branches, though they were the most brittle. As high as she got, she was never satisfied because she could never reach the clouds. Though she swayed with the wind as she clung onto brittle branches, she always wore a smile. There was nothing she was afraid of. She fought lions and taunted the tyrannosaurus rex. She poked sleeping bears and stole gold from dragons. Danger didn't exist in her world. It was all just beautiful chaos and that suited her reckless soul.

Another thing I remember about her is that she was caring. She hated seeing pain and sadness. Wherever she went, she brought laughter to alleviate some of the sorrow that stemmed from life's unfair castigations. She told them stories of cows that fell in love as they sipped on grass cocktails and of how squirrels started stealing shoes to hide their nuts because humans kept cutting down trees and ruining the squirrels' hiding spots. She didn't like how life chastised those who didn't deserve it. If life was a person she would have berated him for causing so much unnecessary pain. I think that is why she built beautiful worlds. She wanted to combat some of the pain in the world even if it was just through silly fiction.

There was only one thing she loved more than clouds. It was the moon. When the clouds went away, she would look out the window and talk to the moon. She saw a Cheshire cat smile in the curvature of the moon and she liked how sometimes, the stars joined in to make a face. The stars were part of most of her bedtime stories. She found gravestones in the blinking lights and she made up massacres. No one ever stayed dead in her world. She had zombies, skeletons, and vampires digging through layers of dirt just to see the moon. They would have graveyard picnics and chat about how alive they felt even though they were dead. Sometimes, the moon would join in. She had a lot to say and with them she had an audience. The girl I knew saw beauty in death and grime and that is near the top of my list of things I miss about her.

I wish I could speak to her again. I would ask her how she always used to believe in herself. She had an obstinance that carried her through every attempt to change her. She knew when she was right and when she was wrong and she knew when to be wrong in order to be right. She had her beliefs and there was never a day that she lived in contradiction with them. Her mind and heart were in sync. She made decisions easily and never second-guessed herself. She believed that all things happen for a reason so she took many risks. Though things didn't always turn out well, she took it in stride because she knew it would all work out in the end. She carried herself with confidence and didn't let anything or anyone stand in her way. I wish I learned how to live like she did.

The funny thing is that she also trusted others. It feels like an oxymoron: to trust yourself and others, but she did it and she did it effortlessly. She lived on a cloud of trust, buoyant on the feeling of content that came from loving herself and others. She melded her dreams with that of others and found a way to propel everyone forward no matter what. Somehow she found the balance between putting herself first while catering to the needs of others. The pendulum swung consistently for her because she learned that in order to love others you have to love yourself.

I don't know exactly when it happened. I can't remember the time or place. Somewhere along crooked lines and spiralling sunsets, I lost her. I still catch glimpses of her from time to time in my periphery but I know she isn't there. No matter how hard I look, I can't find her. I think I could have lost her when I stopped looking at the moon because it stopped glistening for me. Perhaps I lost her when I let stars be stars and when I gave up on graveyard picnics. Or maybe she left because somewhere in her cloud tales, I stopped listening. I can't remember what her last story was. I think it was about a girl with a huge expanse of cotton candy hair that no one could tame. Maybe she left because I tried to tame her. I wish I could remember her last story or at least know why she left because I miss her. I miss her laughter and the beautiful worlds she made. I wish I held on to her. There are so many things I wish I could ask her. I wish she fought to stay. It was supposed to be her and I together forever. I would give anything for just one more story.

I replaced her with someone more cautious. She is level-headed and logical. She fights for herself and treads carefully along known, familiar paths. She second-guesses herself but I don't mind because I know she is afraid of everything. She takes no risks. She studies probabilities and measures outcomes before taking a step forward. She is safety exemplified. There are no surprises in her life. There are no games or adventures through forbidden desires and dangerous dreams. There is routine and normalcy, conformity and obedience. There is a calming air of nothingness surrounding her. It is not beautiful but it is a sterile ambience and I think that is what I need. It is in direct contrast to the unpredictability I had before but like I said, maybe my colourful world would function better if it was a single shade of whatever calm is made of. I will settle for that until I find the chaos I once knew.

As I go through each day with her replacement, I can't help but wish for more. I know calm is what I need. It is what everyone tells me I need. They tell me I will thrive without nonsensical dreams but I don't think they know that those dreams made me want to live. With this boring calm that reeks of conformity, I find the world a hard place to navigate. I think I figured out why I lost her. I gave up on my dreams and with it went wishes on stars and daydreams of dragons. There isn't anything I can do to get her back. I have tried. I will push her to the back of my mind and live as they want me to.

Don't get me wrong. I still think about her, this girl I once knew. I let her get away, the girl I could have been. I regret letting her go without a fight because I need her to go on. She was the best of me and I left her behind. She would hate what I've become. I hate what I've become because I remember being so much more. I will keep looking for her in the clouds and in the stars but for now she lives at the back of my mind where my dreams lie too.

TALIA

~

All the money in the world cannot make up for the embarrassment that comes with a barren womb but the day I was born was still a day of shame for my father. As village chief he had an ego the size of the vibrantly decorated elephants we rode in Jaipur during the Holi Festival. It was a blow to his ego to see that despite what the village sami, a prophet of sorts, had predicted, I was female. He found a way to cope though, by convincing himself that I was his property and someday he would make use of this liability. My mother had protected me from the truth, giving me a childhood void of misogyny and it was her strength that helped me when I needed it most.

When my mother used to comb coconut oil through my hair with her fingers she always had a faraway look in her eyes. She would stare out the window while her fingers formed knots that would end up in two fat braids and when she was done she would wipe her hands on her saree and walk to the stove, still lost in thought.

'What are you thinking about, Amma?' I would ask as I put on my starch-ironed school uniform.

Each time she would smile and say, 'One day you will know, Talia.'

My father would then wander out of my parent's room, rubbing sleep out of his eyes and Amma would rush to the table with a plate of tosai[2] that she had been making since dawn. 'Are those like pancakes, Appa?', I asked one day.

My father growled in my mother's direction saying, 'This is what we get for sending her to a private school. We are paying for them to corrupt her mind with all that Western garbage. She's going to have white men ambitions and then we'll have a problem.'

My mother didn't say a word. She just stood there in her curry-stained saree, not meeting my father's eyes. It took me a while to learn that he never expected her to reply. Her silence was obedience and that is all a husband wants from his wife.

'But why do I have to learn to make sambar[3], Amma?' I asked when I turned thirteen. 'I don't see why I have to learn when I am going to be a doctor one day. All these spices will never matter.'

'One day you will see, Talia,' she said and I grudgingly picked up the ladle and stirred in the lentils. Appa came home from work and sat at the table. Amma brought out a six-dish spread along with the rice and roti[4]. He dug in without acknowledging her presence but by then I was used to it.

When I reached home after school one day, I saw Amma nursing her bruised eye. I knew where it came from so I didn't ask. She caught me staring and said, 'They like to tell us we are nothing, Talia, but the day you believe it is the day they win. You must never let them win. Promise me you will never let them win, Talia.' It was an easy

---

2   A crepe-like dish made of rice. A staple breakfast in India.

3   A curry that is usually eaten with tosai.

4   Flatbread

promise to make but years later I found out how difficult it was to keep.

There were many things Amma never told me, things she hid behind her kohl-painted eyes. The wraps of her saree hid many secrets and behind the neat folds of her pallu[5], she kept scars and hurts that never saw the light of day. Of all the things she never told me the one I felt most betrayed by was the one I found out on my fifteenth birthday. All her cryptic sayings, whispered since I was young, finally made sense that day. She had hidden the fact that a woman dies in more ways than one and the day I pricked my finger on the pin of my wedding saree, I was gone.

As my husband tied the thali[6] around my neck, I felt the noose tighten and when we lay on our wedding sheets and he violated me, I believed that my body was his prerogative because it was no longer my own. The part of me that died meant I was finally of use to my father. For once he was proud of me because I was doing what I was told.

I eventually knew what it was like to merely exist like my mother and her mother before her. All the education I had was buried in the creases of the colourful dyed cloth I had been trained to wrap around myself since I was young. All the dreams of saving a life on an operating table was projected onto working at a stove and serving my husband. I had been trained all my life to be a wife and I was conditioned to be content with that.

Perhaps it was the constant reminder that I was of no

---

5   Part of a saree that hangs over the shoulder.
6   A gold string blessed by loved ones, tied around the bride's neck by the groom. The equivalent of a wedding ring.

use because I was a woman, perhaps it was the compliments on my hair, my face, anything but my intellect, perhaps it was the ease with which he inserted himself into me, ignoring my right to say no that brought me close to breaking my promise to my mother. It was when I was ready to break that promise that I felt a kick in my lower abdomen. I went home to Amma that day and she smiled because she knew that I too had found my saving grace.

Nine months of hope was what I held within me and when a bundle of matted hair and blood was handed to me, I finally had something to call my own. It was in the eyes of my daughter that I found my will to live. As her little hands clung on to me I knew that I owed her the life my mother had tried to give me. My daughter had brought me back to life and for that I would give her the life I never had, fulfilling the promise I made to my mother and to myself. I will never let them win.

THE CONDITIONED SMILE

The act of baring one's teeth is a sign of submission among primates such as apes and monkeys. Sometimes it is an act of aggression to establish dominance and other times, it is used to diffuse tension within the species. The difference lies in the eyes and in other physical gestures that accompany this 'smile'. Humans on the other hand, though we are part of the primate order, bare our teeth when we're happy or at least when we pretend to be. We part our lips and put our slightly imperfect, maize-coloured teeth on display. Some just engineer the muscles in their cheek to contract and form an upward curve with their lips. It is a natural act, to smile when the world gives us something to smile about. The act of smiling is linked to joy, but for her, it is a safety mechanism. It is means of staying alive.

Every day as she leaves her house, she is greeted by the garbage collector. He catcalls her and she gives him a polite smile. She knows that if she doesn't there is a chance that he will follow her. Her car is parked a ways away and she meets many men on her walk. They wolf-whistle and she keeps her head down but she still wears a smile, just in case. She doesn't want to smile but over the years it has become her panic response. I think that's because she was once slapped for not smiling on demand.

'You'll look prettier if you smiled,' the man had said.

She told him that she disagreed. He had grabbed her by her ponytail and slapped her, demanding she smiled. He only stopped when she did. She had walked home, head ringing from all the slaps. That is why she smiles for the same reason primates do. It is a plea to leave her alone.

Sometimes this backfires because men take a smile as an invitation to approach her and violate some part of her. She hasn't quite figured out the configuration, when to smile, where to smile, how to smile and whether to smile at all. It is not an easy thing to ascertain because men don't wear their intentions on their sleeves. There are good men and those that wear the face of one. She couldn't tell one from the other. In trying to figure out how to navigate a man's world, she conditioned herself to smile, not in response to happiness as we are all naturally inclined but in response to a different stimulus. This stimulus is the presence of men. She learned once how Russian physiologist Ivan Pavlov trained a dog to salivate at the sound of a bell by making sure that the dog associated the ringing of a bell with food. She trained herself to smile at the sound of heavyset footsteps approaching her. The difference between her and Pavlov is that she didn't mean to instil this behaviour. For her it happened as a means of survival.

She further cemented this conditioning using B.F. Skinner's theory that the outcome of an action affects the behaviour of an individual. Skinner studied this through his rat experiment where rats were either rewarded with food for hitting a lever or were punished through electrocution or were denied food for displaying unfavourable behaviour. He surmised that actions that result in favourable outcomes were more likely to be repeated. She confirmed that conclusion. Whenever she smiles, she is rewarded with something akin to safety. When she is still approached because of her smile, she is alright with it because at least she isn't being punished with a slap nor is she hit with jokes about it being the time of the month or with derogatory comments about being a heinous bitch that is wound too tight. When she smiles, no one threatens to put a smile on her face while promising that she will like it. She likes not being punished so she smiles, teeth bared and cheekbones straining, from carrying the weight of an insincere smile that she has to hold at the risk of her life.

These days it is rare that she gets told to smile. It used to happen regularly. It happened once as she was waiting at a bus stop after dropping off her car at a mechanic shop where she was also harassed and asked to smile. As she boarded the bus, the bus driver made a joke about the raincloud over her head affecting everyone else's mood. He asked her to smile too and pinched her cheek when she did. He didn't stop there. He slapped her backside as she walked past to get to her seat and he told her that she could board for free any time. She had to keep a smile on her face though she felt like screaming. She was trembling the whole ride home, in fear or anger, she didn't know. She glanced at the other passengers who she knew had heard what happened but they averted their gaze, thus telling her that she was on her own. The bus driver told her goodbye by pinching her backside as she got off the bus and she smiled and thanked him.

She can't remember a time when a smile meant happiness. She can't remember the last time she felt happy. She is filled with dread every time she has to leave her house and her day is filled with fear. She smiles at every man she sees and in her eyes lies panic because though some men just walk by, others linger and she doesn't know what they will do next. She was followed to her office once and had to beg the security guard at the door to help her. The security guard did his job but as his reward he had pushed her against the receptionist desk and had run his hands all over her. She wanted to scream but she was shocked and she couldn't move. The receptionist was seated there but she didn't do a thing. After the guard left, the receptionist apologised and told her that he had a gun. She told the receptionist that she didn't expect her to help anyway because no one ever does.

When she had first heard about animal primates and their bared teeth, she saw herself in them. She believed right away that Darwin's theory of evolution was correct. She believes it because she smiles as an act of submission like her primate family does. No one else she knows does that so she must have inherited that from the apes. She wonders if her animal primate family would help her if they were around when someone asks her to smile. She wonders if they would bare their teeth but instead of cowering in fear, she wonders if they would attack. She muses on these things as she gives the world her smile. It is all one can do when you're alone in a man's world.

SHE IS CLAY

No one remembers where or when it began, her slow descent to nothingness. They don't know they played a hand in turning her to nothing. They helped her build her prison, handing her the bricks. Brick by brick she built while those around her applauded. She lived for the chorus of their praise that stemmed from her obedience. That is why she picked up each brick with enthusiasm and placed it down with anticipation. She built solid walls, not a brick out of place. Their encouragement spurred her on. They helped her build her prison then left her all alone. No one remembers where or when it began, no one except for her.

The first brick landed when she was reminded of her uselessness. She was young and they gave her dolls. They didn't teach her how to read or write. She only learned to play pretend. She was good at it. It's a game she continued to play all her life. The next brick landed when she was taught to wash clothes by the river. She got her own basin and she loved when they complimented her on how well she scrubbed. The neighbours' kids used to join her. The third and fourth brick landed when she gave up on her dreams. She realised pursuing what she wanted would mean disappointing those around her. By then she was taught that to live is to please and she pinned her existence on compliments and applause. After that the bricks landed more easily.

The more they encouraged her the faster she laid the bricks. She couldn't see the wall forming. She didn't see the world disappearing. The applause was deafening so it was easy to ignore the voice within, the voice that was begging her to stop, a voice she wouldn't recognise even if she heard it. Those around her didn't care about her but she didn't know that. She didn't know that they saw her as clay to be moulded. She didn't know that they too were once like her. They didn't know any better. They too craved approval and so they too built walls. She continued to lay bricks and they continued to applaud. It was a cycle they were all too familiar with. She lost herself with every brick placed and the applause was her only company. Well, that and bricks.

When she realised what had happened it was too late. She was surrounded by walls with no means of escape. She sat behind these walls and tried to map out a life but she had no tools except bricks and cement. All she could do was build. She tried to climb but she never learned how. She asked them for a ladder but they didn't know what that was for. They were content in their prison and never thought to escape. She started to claw at the walls she was taught to build but nothing she did left a dent. They were right to applaud her because she had built the perfect wall.

She took her life the day the praises died. She couldn't hear them over the dense bricks. Or that is what she told herself. In truth, they stopped clapping when she became all that they wanted her to be. She was miserable like them and thus she was perfect. She slammed her head against the bricks and every hit was one hit closer to freedom, she thought. She thought she would hear their praise again but all she saw was a brick wall, now stained with blood. She realised too late that they applauded her to her demise and she had welcomed it. None of the bricks she had laid could help her. She had put up no resistance because no one ever taught her how to, for they never learnt themselves. She had thrived on approval so when the applause died, she followed.

They were surprised at her death because she seemed content. They couldn't see what could have possibly gone wrong.

'She was flawless,' they said. Obedient to her detriment was what they meant.

They couldn't see why someone who had everything would give it all away. They didn't see that she had nothing at all. They called it a tragedy not knowing that she had died a long time ago. They didn't know they had a hand in it. They didn't know that they took her life the day they handed her that first brick. They robbed her of a life and didn't even shed a tear for they didn't know they killed her. With their brick wall came ignorance and they lived a bliss-filled existence brimming with it.

Perhaps if someone had offered her a hand to remove the bricks she placed she wouldn't have joined the countless others that met the same demise, for there were many who had tried to scale the brick wall but fell short and gave up. Perhaps if one of them were brave enough to tell her that the end was a prison made of moulded mud, then her end wouldn't have been the same. Perhaps if someone had taught her how to make a world of her own, free of applause but filled with all things her, then she wouldn't have felt alone when the crowd was gone and with it her spirit. Perhaps if she had known that that was an option, she would have been something instead of the nothing she became.

Her eulogy told of her nothingness for no one truly knew her, not even herself. No one could remember anything about her. They even forgot her name. They buried her and not a tear was shed. She lived and died a slate written on by others, leaving no marks of her own. They moulded her like clay and left their creation to her own devices. And like a clay pot she broke and no one was there to pick up the pieces.

INTROSPECT

On wishing I knew more
than I know now

THE SIN OF SKIN

What does a naked woman who begs on the sidewalk, a young girl who walks to school alone, a woman who sells her body for a living, a nun who carries a rosary made of silver roses, and a woman who owns a boutique have in common? The answer lies at the end of this story.

I know a woman who roams the streets in nothing but her skin. She begs for money at traffic stops and in front of churches. She sleeps in dark alleys on a mattress made of old newspapers and uses garbage bags filled with food waste as her pillow. She greets me every morning as I leave for work and I give her some money. I don't know how old she is or where she is from. Some say she lost her family in a fatal accident. They say that she never recovered. They tell me that she walks around naked because she lost her mind when she lost her family. She doesn't seem mentally disabled in any way. She seems happy.

Something happened to her recently and I don't know why no one seems to care. I don't know exactly what happened but I do know that she screamed for help and that no one came. She is different from the person she was. She doesn't look up at the sound of coins hitting the bottom of the soup tin. She doesn't smile and she doesn't greet me. She wraps newspapers around her body and fastens them on with mud. I try to speak to her but I think she is tired of telling her story. When I ask those around me about what happened to her, they tell me that she deserves what she got for walking around without clothes. I tell them that she wasn't doing anyone any harm. They tell me that she is lucky she was only raped because most of the time people like her are murdered. They aren't interested in catching her rapist because they say it is her fault. I can't believe they think she is the one who lost her mind.

I know a girl who walks to school every morning. We take the same route. She has her hair up in a long braid and it bounces off her school bag as she practically skips down the sidewalk. This is her first year walking to school on her own. Her mother used to accompany her and I don't know why she stopped but the girl doesn't seem to have a problem with it. As we walk, she tells me about all her friends and about all the fun they have. She fills my silent morning with laughter and gives me something to look forward to. My favourite sight is that of her running to her friends the moment she reaches the school gate. I hear them laugh and I remember a time when I too was like them. She makes me wish that I could go back to school because it's been a while since I've been excited about anything.

Something happened to her recently. It made her lose the spring in her step. She cut her hair short and now her mother accompanies her. She only says hello to me when her mother prompts her to. I don't know exactly what happened. All I heard was that she had been walking to school for extra-curricular activities in the early afternoon alone and that she was wearing shorts when it happened. Everyone I speak to is blaming her mother for letting her go alone. They call her irresponsible and tell her that it is her fault. I think they are forgetting a very important person who is actually at fault in all this but they ignore me when I bring that up. Everyone who tells me the story also seems to focus on the fact that the girl was wearing shorts.

'It's not appropriate for girls to be showing that much skin. What did she expect would happen?' they say.

I tell them that the shorts that girls wear to school are not the problem but they are loud in admonishing the girl so they don't hear me. Whatever happened to her has made the school change the dress code for sports. The girls now wear track pants. It reminds me of when my grandmother yelled at me for wearing shorts in front of my uncles when I was younger. She made me change into track pants too. I don't know how to feel about the fact that nothing has changed in twenty years.

I know a woman who works the streets. She wears fishnet stockings and crop tops as she waves at passers-by. Not many wave back. She is there all day doing her job. Everyone knows how a transaction with her works. It works like every other job. She gets paid for her services and she demands payment upfront before services are rendered. I think that's smart because I have a feeling she wouldn't get paid otherwise. She is shamed by other women daily. She is spat at and treated like she is diseased. She tells them that at least she is doing a job that she likes. They don't believe her. *Who could be happy selling their body*, they think as they walk by, not realising that they too have sold themselves but for much less. She laughs at their misery while they pity her for what they call her misfortune. The men are different from their wives. They don't think she is disgusting until after they get what they pay for. They tease her and flirt with her as they walk by and she tells them her rates. Some pinch her backside and slap it as they go on their way. She doesn't like that but she can't do anything about it.

Something happened to her recently. The police found her dead in a drain that was clogged up with garbage. They only found her because they were cleaning the drain as the place had begun to flood. I don't think anyone noticed that she was missing for a few days. Or maybe they did but they didn't care. They still don't care. They don't care about how she was choked to death after she was raped or the fact that there is a murderer out there. They do care about what she was when she was alive. They gossip about her promiscuity, calling her a slut, and say that this is the only end for people like her. The picture in the newspaper shows her in her fishnet stockings, midriff showing, the rest of her covered in trash. It gives them more ammunition. They blame her lifestyle and body for everything. They say she ended up where she belongs.

I know a woman who works in the church. She carries rosary beads and dresses in a button-down blouse and a skirt that goes down to her calves. Sometimes she wears a matching headscarf. She lives in a terrace connected to the church with her other holy sisters. I hear that she sits in the chapel all day and that she attends all masses. I suppose that is her job. Sometimes our paths cross as I am going to work and she wishes me a blessed morning. Once, she gave me my own rosary made of silver roses. I carry it with me and it makes me feel safe. She always tells me to join her in church when I can. I haven't taken her up on that offer. I have seen her stop and talk to the beggar woman who now wears newspapers and mud for clothes. The beggar woman ignores her but the nun just smiles. I wonder what it is like to live the life of a nun, to answer to no one but God. It doesn't seem like an easy life but I see this woman smile and I think that maybe it isn't so bad.

Something happened to her recently and now the sisters walk in pairs. They wear longer skirts. They now cover their ankles. Headscarves are now compulsory for them. I don't understand why. They hold umbrellas when they go to church regardless of the weather, even though they live next door. They didn't used to carry umbrellas, just rosary beads and a smile. They don't carry a smile anymore. No one knows what happened to her but they say that she may be pregnant. They also say that she doesn't speak anymore. I hear people talk about how she shouldn't have gone out alone. They say that God should have saved her. Somehow I thought that with her it would be different. I thought they would care about finding her rapist. Instead they find some way to blame her for not taking precautions. They say that men like forbidden fruit and that she presented them with temptation. I want to believe that they aren't talking about her ankles but I think they are. They call her impure. They say that she was punished by God. They say that if she is pregnant then she has fallen from grace and should leave the convent. They wonder if she will keep the baby. I guess everyone loves to play God and pass judgment. It seems to be the only thing they know how to do.

I am a woman who works at a boutique. I take the same route every morning down the same street. I am sometimes accompanied by a woman and her daughter. Her daughter used to walk to school alone. I say hello to the beggar woman and give her enough money for lunch. She used to sit around naked. Now she wears mud. As I pass by I see nuns in pairs holding umbrellas, marching into the church. They don't stop to tell me to have a blessed morning. They don't tell me to join them when I can. I wish I took up their offer before. I walk past the church and down the street where a woman in fishnets used to stand. She made the boring sidewalk interesting. Now it is dull and I walk alone.

Something happened to me recently but I refuse to tell anyone about it. I know what they will do. I know what they will say. They will blame the way I dress and say that I invited it. They never approved of my tight skirts and cleavage so this will only give them satisfaction. They will say that the sight of my ankles beckoned him and that I should have known better. I will never understand how they can believe that. I do know though that nothing will be done to find him. I have to deal with this by myself. I get pepper spray and a knife. I don't wear skirts anymore. I hope it is enough. My daily routine has changed since that day. I now scrub at my skin daily to remove him but all it does is open the wounds from the day before. It's fine though, because the scars are hidden under my new clothes.

So, what does a naked woman who begs on the side-walk, a young girl in her sports attire, a woman who sells her body for a living, a nun who carries a rosary made of silver roses, and a woman who owns a boutique have in common? Did you guess the answer? There is no prize if you did. There are no winners in this game, only sinners and skin.

THE RUNAWAY BRIDE

She wore red the day she ran from everything she ever knew. She decided to run because her wedding had been planned. This was a disaster for a girl who had a twenty-year plan.

She had a plan for every day ever since she turned twelve. She made lists of things she had to get done and she made sure that each box was ticked before she went to bed. She knew where she wanted to be in life, every step of the way and she worked towards that. Everything usually went according to her plan. She had become the first woman hired as a neurosurgeon. She was the youngest one too. Everyone was surprised. Everyone but her. It was all according to her plan. She planned every moment of her life. Hell, she even knew the names of her children and she planned where they would go to school. That was fifteen years down the line though and a wedding only came in at the ten-year mark in her plans. Not knowing what to do, she decided to run. She knew she had to if she were to salvage her plans.

She had penned out fourteen opportunities to run. She divided the opportunities into two periods, A.D. (Ante Disaster) and P.D. (Post Disaster), the disaster being her wedding day.

In the A.D. her first opportunity to run came when she

was preparing for the engagement ceremony. Her parents knew she did not want to get married so in all the days leading up to the ceremony, she was monitored by one of her hundreds of relatives. However, on the day of her engagement, in all the rush to get everything ready, they left her alone. She wasn't prepared to execute the plan though because she hadn't packed her bags. She didn't expect to be left alone. That failure was on her. She sat through a ceremony that consisted of her father giving the groom's father permission to proceed with the wedding. She would have dissented but she couldn't even speak because she was reeling from her lack of preparation.

Her second opportunity came that same day as the engagement party went on. She had rushed home after the ceremony and grabbed a suitcase. She filled it with anything she could fit in. She hid the suitcase under her vanity set. It was a good hiding place because she was expected to sit there as they adorned her. The women in her household and those related to her husband-to-be were all there to get her ready. They didn't notice the suitcase amongst all the chaos. This second opportunity was a futile one because there wasn't a moment where she was left alone. She was being monitored. It was just what women did when weddings take place. They talked and laughed as they all got ready in the same space. There was no room to stand, let alone run.

At the party she was the centre of attention. She was pulled ten ways as everyone sang and danced. She met her future in-laws and they were nice but they weren't part of the plan. As those around her partied, she looked for all possible exits. Unfortunately, they needed her for every ritual that took place. She was handed a written vow to present to her future husband and he gave her one in return. She didn't know what it said but she didn't care. She only cared that all this wrecked her plans. The wedding date was set based on her and her husband-to-be's birth dates. Their parents were given possible dates based on their astrology signs. Her parents chose the earliest one, two months and three days from the date of the engagement party. She exchanged rings with her betrothed and that was the end of that plan.

The moment the date was announced, she calculated the amount of time she had to make her escape. One thousand five hundred and thirty-two hours. To anyone else that would be ample time but for her it was no time at all. She was used to planning years in advance. She checked for plane tickets and had alternative means of making her escape. She had the number of multiple cab companies. She considered sending her luggage ahead of her but she didn't know where to go. That was one part of her plan that she couldn't figure out. She had the money but no destination in mind.

The days leading up to the wedding passed swiftly. She had dress fittings, wedding reception decisions to make, relatives to meet, guest lists to approve, and she was called in for work at odd hours. She feigned interest in all things wedding related because not doing so would be suspicious. She couldn't deny though that it was fun. Planning was one of her favourite things and with a wedding, there was tons to plan. She loved the rush of ticking things off a list.

Before long it was time for the wedding. Fortunately for her it was a three day affair. For the span of three days she planned nine instances to make her escape. The first was before the purification ceremony. It was a ceremony where she and her betrothed were to be smothered in a turmeric paste and sprinkled with various oils by married women for protection from spirits. As she was getting into her car, she got a call from her betrothed who asked if he could accompany her to the ceremony. She had no choice but to agree. They spoke during the car ride and she was surprised that she was not repulsed by him. She found him pleasant and engaging. The ceremony went on and she enjoyed herself. She told herself she couldn't leave because, covered in yellow turmeric paste, they would find her right away. It was a small town after all.

The third instance when she could have escaped was as she was leaving for her bridal shower the day before the wedding. She told her friends that she would drive to the venue but they insisted on accompanying her. They sang folk songs as she drove, her luggage in the boot. The bridal shower took hours. Her friends and cousins applied henna in floral motifs to her hands and feet as they spoke about what a marriage entailed and what she had to do as a wife. They told her that the darker the henna was when the paste dried and was washed off, the more her husband would love her. She didn't understand the correlation between the paste and love so she just let them talk. They also applied henna among themselves as part of the ceremony. They had a sleepover at her place. Needless to say, she didn't run.

On the day of her wedding, she set her alarm to leave right on time to catch the first bus to the airport. She was running out of time to execute her A.D. plans. Her bags were packed, neatly this time. Her mother had helped her because she would be moving out to live with her husband after the ceremony. The only thing that stood in her way was the countless people who were up early too. They brought her breakfast and gave her their blessings before helping her to get dressed. They showed her the wedding clothes, a red saree adorned with faux diamonds. They draped it on her and put on other accoutrements. Then they fussed over her hair and makeup. She let them do whatever they wanted. She was biding her time.

As time passed, she began to panic. She had many plans and no time at all. She yelled at everyone to leave the room and they did. She was the bride and they didn't want to ruin her day. She didn't hesitate for a moment. Throwing her bag out the window, she climbed out and used the piping to get down. As she was putting her luggage into the car, she was stopped.

'I was just checking to see if everything I need is here,' she said and they believed her. They did wait to escort her back into the house though so perhaps the lie wasn't as convincing as she thought.

Her next plan was foolish. She knew it too. She planned to sneak off during the groom's arrival. She thought she could blend into the crowd and walk away but, in red, she stood out. She wandered off slowly but the crowd was made up of people who knew her. They walked her back to her father who was getting ready to give her away. It was just moments before the giving-away ceremony that she ran. She excused herself to use the restroom and took a detour. She lifted her saree up to her knees and ran as fast as she could to the nearest bus stop, her heavy earrings tugging at her earlobes, threatening to rip them. She had her keys and according to her plan, she could get home before anyone realised she was gone.

She wore red the day she ran from everything she ever

knew but she didn't get far. Her last plan in the A.D. failed. You can't run away in a small town. The bus driver got a phone call and turned around. They dragged her back to the altar where she sat through prayers and rice throwing. It was a beautiful ceremony. She knew it would be because she planned it. She would have enjoyed it if she actually wanted to be there. As she looked around for a way to run, she saw that each exit was blocked off by one of her family members. She gave up for the moment and went through with the ceremony. She exchanged flower garlands with her betrothed and their garments were tied together as they circumnavigated the fire in the middle of the dais. She was given a necklace that was fastened on by her husband and as they were showered with rice, she got ready to execute the next phase of her plan.

She had drawn up Post Disaster (P.D.) plans so all she had to do was wait to execute them. As they marked her as a married woman with red dye down her middle-parted hairline, her P.D. plans were set in motion. She planned to run before they left for their new home. If that didn't work, she would run in the middle of the night. She had a plan of escape for every day and every situation. She didn't know that she wouldn't get away or that her long-term plans would never come to fruition. It wasn't because she was held back. She had all the freedom she wanted in her new home. It was because something happened when she got married, something that made her change her plans. For all her planning, she didn't factor in falling in love.

'I'll leave the doors unlocked,' her husband had said when they were alone that first night. She asked him why.

'In case you want to run,' he said. He smiled and she felt her heart race. She had never felt that way before. She knew she wasn't repulsed by him from their conversation during the ride to the purification ceremony but she didn't think she would find him more than pleasant. As the days went on she found him agreeable, funny, and witty. She looked forward to his smile and he made her laugh. Slowly, her plans to run in the P.D. shifted and disappeared. After all, she never did have a destination in mind. And now she couldn't think of a place she'd rather be than by his side.

She shuffled her plans. Both long-term and short-term now included him in them. She didn't mind that he had ruined her plans because she found herself happier. Everything fell into place like it usually does when love is part of the equation. Just when it was all going according to her new plan, life gave her another pleasant surprise but that is a story for another time.

MONSTERS IN THE MOONLIGHT

I used to love the moon. I loved the moon so much that my parents bought me a book on moon facts. I memorised the facts on each page. I knew from a young age that the moon was a natural satellite, though I didn't know what a satellite was. I'm still not sure what it is. I knew that people weighed less on the moon and that the moon borrowed its light from the sun. No one knew why I loved the moon. I think I loved it because it was my only company on long trips to my grandma's house. In the backseat of an old Chevrolet Trailblazer, I found comfort in the rays that followed me on my journey. It felt like the moon and I had a secret, like we were on an adventure that no one knew about but us.

That is the last time I remember feeling safe at the sight of the moon. Now, a feeling of dread looms as soon as the sun sets. I don't fear the darkness that night brings but I do fear what the darkness shrouds and envelops. It is the monsters that come out as soon as daylight ends that I fear. The moon feels like a stranger, co-conspiring with the monsters, shining her rays on me while her friend, the darkness, hides the vile creatures. That is why I no longer trust the moon. I am now friends with the sun.

I have never faced one of these monsters but others like me have. Those who live to tell their tales say that the monsters are merciless and that they take what they want. They say that these creatures mutilate and violate you while the moon watches. They say that they didn't see the monsters coming because of the darkness. They tell of gruff hands grabbing them and warning them to be silent. They say that they remember the same hands around their throat. Sometimes it is a knife. The scariest part, they say, is that you can never tell who the monster is. They hide in plain sight. They walk around in daylight. Sometimes sunlight deters them, sometimes it doesn't. In the sunlight these monsters look like your friends but when darkness comes, you see the monsters they truly are. I learned from survivors that I cannot trust anyone, not even the moon.

Today I have to do something I usually avoid. I have to go out in the dark. Alone. I used to go out alone all the time when I was younger. I used to walk home from school alone. I used to walk home from my friend's house after a long day of pretending that we studied. I walked to the football field to meet my friends on weekends. Now I don't feel safe being outside. I have made every excuse I can think of not to go but no one seems to hear me. They always have something to say in reply, in their condescending, patronising tones. They don't understand my apprehension about the night-time because they don't have to worry about monsters. because they are either the monsters themselves or they are friends with them. They pretend they don't understand why I fear the darkness but I know they do, they just don't care.

I have to get ready hours in advance because there is a lot of prep to do before I can walk out the door. I take out my loosest clothes, a tracksuit to wear on top of my dress and I stuff my heels in my bag. Heels aren't optimum for running. Then I work on my hair. I usually spend time styling it but today I have to stuff my hair under a beanie so the monsters don't have anything to grab if they chase me. I won't make it easy for them. I stuff my pockets with pepper spray, one in each pocket and I also carry my pocketknife. I have a small alarm which I can set off but, based on incident reports, those aren't effective because no one is willing to help. I manage to fit a small flashlight in too. Finally, before I leave, I stuff my bag which contains my shoes, into my tracksuit top to look bulky. I look in the mirror and I see someone who will not draw attention. I send a message to my mum with information on where I'm going and the route I will be taking before finally opening the door.

I make sure the door is locked. I check it three, maybe four more times before leaving. Holding my key between my fingers like a claw, I leave the safety of my house. It sounds like a dreadful thing to do but I think being assaulted and dying is worse. The streetlights aren't lit and it's not surprising. No matter how many times the women have complained about it, it's never fixed. I assumed it would get done considering many women have been attacked but I think even if someone died, nothing would get done.

As I walk I keep an eye on my surroundings. These are the times I wish humans had panoramic vision. You would think women at least would have evolved that characteristic since we have to be wary of threats from all angles. Instead I have to turn around to make sure I'm not being followed and that in itself draws attention. Another one of my senses that I have to rely on heavily when I go out is hearing. When I was younger I used to put on headphones and blast my music as I went out for a walk but I learned from assault survivors that I need to keep an ear out for anything because the darkness hides monsters. I learned that don't have the luxury of moonlight strolls. How naïve I was to believe that I would be able enjoy the moonlight.

The further away from home I get, the more paranoid I become. I used to want to feel as carefree as the women in period dramas did when they went on walks but now I know that the fact that they were out alone and didn't face any danger is the greatest indication their stories were fiction. I run through all the self-defence training I got from my mother as I walk. She taught me the best places to punch to get away. I know how to break a zip tie and how to dodge attacks. I learned how to break a nose and my mother was the first one to tell me to carry my key. My hand cramps from holding the key so tightly and I loosen my grip. I check my pockets for the pepper spray and I make sure my knife is easily accessible. All it takes is one mistake, one moment of distraction, to become a headline or another face in the obituary section.

The light of the full moon shines down on me and I pull my hoodie over my head. Unwillingly, I think of women just like me who have walked down dark alleys and broken paths that led into the unknown and how most never came out the other side. It is not a picture I need in my head at this moment but it comes to me nevertheless. They probably took the same precautions I did but the moon let them down. The darkness did too. It didn't shroud them in its protection. They had to protect themselves and failed. Everyone and everything let them down.

I reach my destination and I rush to the door. The fear leaves me as I am let in. I excuse myself to use the restroom and I remove my layers of clothes and adjust my hair to look presentable. I change out of my running shoes into my heels. I transfer the pepper spray and pocketknife to my handbag and keep the other bottle of pepper spray in my dress pocket. I can't be too careful. After all, most women know their attacker. I send a message to my mother and let her know that I reached my destination safely. I tell her I will let her know when I leave. The meeting goes on but I can't concentrate on anything. All I am thinking about is my walk home. It will be darker then, the monsters' favourite time to come out.

The meeting goes by without a hitch. At least, I think it did. I excuse myself again to put on my tracksuit and I change my shoes and tuck my hair away. It doesn't take long because I have had plenty of practice over the years. I send my mother a message before saying goodbye to everyone. I see them try to hide their smiles. They think I am paranoid but none of them are women. They don't know what it's like to walk home at night in fear that they might not make it back. Some volunteer to walk me back, I instinctively decline. They may be offering out of the goodness of their heart but I cannot take that risk. It could cost me my life.

I go through the same steps again. I have my key in one hand and the other is in my pocket clinging to my knife. I jump at any shadow and curse at the moon for not being a bigger help. I run through my list of defences and as I get closer to my house, I run. I have my key ready and I quickly open the door and get in. I don't hesitate to lock the door and as usual I check three or four times to make sure that it is locked. I only breathe easy after checking the house for intruders. Somewhere out there someone didn't make it home. Today it wasn't me. I fear that someday it will be. I fear that someday my name will be just another headline. I fear that it is inevitable.

GROWING JASMINES

In a mess of a town overrun by potholes and muddy puddles, over the sound of car honks and clamorous vendors, the squeals of a newborn were barely heard. It wasn't the outside sounds though that were drowning him out. It was the screams of fifteen women in the shared maternity ward. Some were still in the initial stages of pushing while others could feel something push through. Amidst the noise, the newborn met his mother.

Before she had a chance to hold him, his grandmother took him from the nurse and rushed out the door. He was welcomed with cheers from his father and all his father's brothers, his father's father and all his father's father's brothers. They commented on how he resembled his grandfather and paraded him around town. All the while, in the corner of the maternity ward, his mother was sewn back together. She was in pain and couldn't see straight but she was elated that she had carried out her duty.

She went through the same thing a year later, then two years after that. She had twin boys following her first three children and the cheers were even louder then. She never had a chance to hold any of her babies until they were handed back to her to be fed but she didn't mind that. She knew what she was there for. Being ripped apart and sewn back together wasn't pleasant but she did it because of the happiness it brought her husband. He was proudest of her when she was carrying his sons. He liked to be with her and he took her to meet his friends when she was at her roundest. Even though she could barely walk and was exhausted, she let strangers feel her abdomen as her husband bragged about his sons. She liked how he almost seemed to care for her. She never had that luxury when she wasn't pregnant. He barely noticed her until he needed her in bed.

When her sixth child was born, something was different. There were no cheers and no one carried the newborn out to meet the family. In fact, this was the first child that they let her hold. She rested the child against her and saw that the baby had her eyes and when it stretched its little lips she saw that it was her smile. She asked her mother-in-law to take the baby to see its father but the woman told her that they would not be interested in seeing it. She asked the old woman why and the woman said, 'She is nothing special.' The newborn was left alone with her mother and for once it was easy for her to bear the pain of being sewn together because her daughter was there to accompany her.

She was allowed to do many things she couldn't before. They even let her name the child. She chose the name Mallikai after her favourite flower, the jasmine. She always loved the scent of jasmine as she pinned a cluster of it in her hair. It reminded her of home and of the days when she wasn't afraid. Her little jasmine bud was her new home. With her she was a little less afraid. No one took issue with the name, mostly because they didn't care. She didn't care what they thought either. She had her little jasmine bud with her and that was all she needed.

None of the villagers visited her at home like they usually did. There were no fruit baskets or pots of herbal remedies. No one congratulated her husband and that only made him angry. He was more irritable than he ever was and he snapped at her more. She did her best to ensure that there was nothing to complain about but he always found something. He yelled when his morning masala tea was too hot. When she had gone to cool the tea down, he picked up the tumbler and flung it at her before leaving for work. He scolded her when he didn't like the shirt she had ironed for him though he didn't use to mind her choices before. To stop him from getting angry over the shirts, she began having multiple shirts ready for him. It didn't matter though. He always found something to yell about.

When he was angry, she made sure to keep the little girl away from him because she only seemed to make it worse. Whenever the baby cried, he would say, 'Is that the only thing she is good for? Noise?' Her sons were the same. She didn't like how at such a young age they had begun to sound like their father but it wasn't her place to correct them. They yelled at the little girl when she cried so she kept the baby away from them. The household was split in two, her husband and his sons, and her and her daughter. Though she was yelled at and scalded with hot tea, her little girl always managed to put a smile on her face.

Her mother-in-law and her mother came to visit almost six months after the baby was born. They insisted on staying with the family after the sons were born but they seemed to forget that the little girl even existed. They didn't clamber to hold her like they did with the boys. They came with bags of gifts and the woman had hoped that maybe they would have gotten something for the little girl but all the toys were for the boys. They ignored the baby even when she cried. They even told the woman to ignore the child, as that is how it will learn to be independent. She remembered how they never let her sons cry for even a moment. She decided to do the same for her daughter. Her little girl would not cry.

With her little girl she had many firsts. She never had the chance to see any of her sons start to crawl. She was always in the kitchen preparing treats for the guests who never stopped pouring in. No one was there to celebrate with her when her daughter began to crawl. There were no photos taken, no phone calls to all their relatives. Her husband didn't even notice. She did though, and she rushed to the baby and hugged the baby so tight she began to squirm. She was there helping the girl to walk and teaching her to talk. She used her sons' old books and a small blackboard to teach the girl to write. They were both covered in chalk by the end of it.

She smiled and laughed for the first time in a long while. She took out her sewing machine that she hadn't touched in years and made the prettiest dresses for the little girl. Although she wanted to give her daughter everything, she couldn't because her husband never gave her permission to buy anything.

'It is a waste of money,' he would say when she dared to ask. She didn't ask him why it wasn't a waste of money when he splurged on his sons. She knew the answer. It was an answer she had heard from her father too.

'Boys are an investment. Girls are good for nothing. You can ask your husband for nice things when you are older,' he had said when she asked him why her brother could always have new shoes for school.

Her mother had agreed with him. She said, 'If you give a girl a little, she will want more. That is dangerous. She will be pampered then no one will want to marry her.' She got nothing from her parents except a wedding dowry. It was the first time they gave her something. Even then, it wasn't for her. They had handed her husband's family a tray laden with gold jewellery and handed her off to them as if getting rid of festering carrion.

She began saving money for her daughter the moment she realised that her husband would have a dowry for the girl and nothing else. Each time she was given monthly allowances for groceries, she put aside a small portion for the girl. When her husband refused to get her a school uniform, she bought one for her. When he only wanted to pay for half the girl's books, she paid the rest. She protected her daughter the way she wished her mother protected her. She remembered how she used to go to school with a badly sewn pinafore and how she never made friends because they thought she was poor. She remembered how she was embarrassed by the teachers in front of all her classmates when she told them that she didn't have her books. Her daughter didn't have to experience that because of her.

She took her daughter on train rides and boat rides. She took her to the marketplace and showed her the things her mother showed her. She taught the girl how to cook, sew, garden, and buy groceries. Unlike her mother though, she didn't remind the girl that she needed to know these things so her husband wouldn't leave her. She didn't bully the girl like her mother did. She didn't pick on her at every turn or constantly tell her how she would never be good enough for any man. She only showed the girl love and she got it back in return.

The day the girl began to bleed was the first time her father paid attention to her. She was fourteen. They had a lavish ceremony, celebrating her maturity. He invited all the people in town and spared no expense. He bought her the most exuberant sarees and jewellery. He hired musicians and bought trays of sweet treats for the guests. The girl was excited to be acknowledged for once. She didn't know that he wanted to let the town know that she was ready to become a bride. He was getting ready to pass her on to someone else.

The girl didn't recognise any of the guests who arrived but they pinched her cheeks with their stubby fingers and said, 'What a beautiful girl.' It made her mother's skin crawl to see her daughter handled like merchandise. She saw how the women in the room watched the girl as she spoke. They commented on her physique and her long hair. They marvelled at her eyes but they didn't like how much she spoke. They followed her with their eyes all through the evening and by the end of the night it seemed like they had all come to a decision. The woman had come to a decision too. She had been forced into married at fifteen. Her daughter would not be forced into anything.

Marriage proposals began arriving at the house just days after the ceremony. There were photos of the suitors attached and all of them looked at least ten years older than the girl. Sensing that someday soon her husband would accept one of the proposals, she gathered all the jewellery she had and sold it all. She added the money to what she had already saved. She began taking weekly trips to the train station with the girl and taught her how to buy her own train ticket. She took the girl on different routes until the girl was familiar with all the paths. She showed her places she had never dared wander. She showed her jasmine what the world could give her outside of the small dusty town. She gave her daughter what she wished her mother had given her.

She saw fear in her little girl's eyes the day her father told her that she was to be married. The girl had looked at her mother as if asking why she was letting this happen. Hugging her child, she told her that everything would work out in the end.

The girl was taken to buy sarees with her future mother-in-law and she met her future husband whom she disliked immediately. She didn't like the way his eyes ran up and down her body. All the while her mother reminded her that everything would be fine. She believed her mother. She had protected her all her life and she knew that she would do it again.

She was starting to lose hope as the engagement proceeded according to plan. She had expected her mother to object but she did nothing except assure her that all would be well. Though she couldn't see how that could be, she trusted her mother. Even after the wedding hall was booked, invitations sent out and her wedding garments chosen, she had faith that her mother would come through. She was right to have faith.

The night before the wedding her mother came to her and told her what she was to do. She handed her train tickets and gave her the schedule for each train.

'They won't be able to stop you. I will stall them,' she told her daughter. She handed the girl all the money she had saved for fourteen years, along with the money she had gotten for her jewellery. She told the girl to take her wedding jewellery with her too. There was enough money there for the girl to buy a house and live comfortably for years. She asked her mother why she wasn't coming with her.

'I need to stall them,' she said.

'Will I ever see you again?' she asked and her mother told her she didn't think so.

'Then I don't want to go,' the girl said.

'You must go. You can do better than this place. You can study and get a job you love. Find someone you love and marry when you want. You must go,' she told her daughter. Her heart shattered as she told her daughter to go but she knew that if the girl stayed she would have to watch her heart break every day of her life.

She spent her last night with her daughter. She told the girl how much she loved her and made her promise that no matter what, she would not return. They spoke for hours, as if trying to fit in all the words they wouldn't be able to say after that night. There was not enough time or words, but they made do.

After everyone had left for the temple, she ran. She had insisted on being alone with her mother and though it wasn't customary, they let her. Saying goodbye to her little girl was the most difficult thing she ever had to do. She looked at her daughter's smile though and remembered how ever since she was born, her little jasmine bud had brought her nothing but happiness. It was her turn to do something for her.

She drove the girl to the train station and even though she wanted to wait with her until her train arrived, she had to play her part. She hugged her daughter for the last time and told her she loved her. She left her heart in that station and her daughter took it with her as she boarded her train.

As the mother got in the car and drove to the temple in the middle of town she stopped herself from crying by thinking about how happy her daughter would be. She could take anything when she thought about her daughter's smile. It was her daughter's smile that stayed on her mind as she drove to her demise.

She arrived at the temple and was met by her sons. They asked her where the girl was. She told them that she didn't know. Her answer was met with a slap from her husband. Her head rang but she focused on her daughter's face. They continued to question her but she told them that she didn't know anything. The other relatives came out of the temple when they heard the commotion and when they heard that the girl was gone they blamed her mother for it. They undid her saree and her sons tied her up so she wouldn't be able to run. They began by slapping her as they questioned her. When she still refused to say anything, they began to punch her. They beat her till her ribs cracked as other relatives cheered them on. Her husband broke her nose and the women pulled at her hair, yelling at her to tell them where the girl went. They told her that they would stop if she told them where the girl went. She didn't make a sound. She had seen how unhappy life with someone she didn't love could be. She had seen what a life as a woman in this town entailed and she decided that she didn't want that for her daughter. Her little jasmine deserved better. She deserved a life full of choices and love. It was the only gift she could give her.

They say she died when her broken rib punctured her heart. The woman who had nothing from the day she was born died with nothing but her daughter's love. It was the most valuable thing she had to call her own. She

watched as a train departed in the distance before she
closed her eyes. She had saved her little jasmine bud to
bloom another day.

JUST ANOTHER DAY IN MAY

I might die today. I feel the blood flow as I lie here. Every time I try to move I feel a tug in my gut so I stay still and wait until the pain passes. It is not the kind of pain that fades quickly, like poking a balloon and watching it bounce back, no dent in sight. It is like a metal rod dipped in flames has seared my skin and long after it has gone, I still feel the heat as my skin melts.

The blood feels warm. It isn't flowing anymore. I feel cold. My fingers feel cold. My feet do too. I try to warm my fingers by tucking them underneath me but I move too much and the stabbing pain in my gut intensifies. I feel a little spurt of blood and I stop. I want to call for help but there is no one home. I reach in my pocket to take my phone out but it isn't there. I threw it aside earlier. I know I flung it toward the window so I turn my head and I see it. I reach for it with my cold fingers but it is just out of reach. I try to move closer to it, slowly shifting my weight and sliding but all I manage to do is push my phone further away. It's no use anyway. I'll bleed out before anyone can get here.

I wonder what will happen at my funeral. I can't remember if I told anyone if I'd rather be buried or cremated. I have always hated tight spaces. I used to have this recurring dream that I was being crushed by a giant wheel and

I would wake up with my heart thumping. I think being buried would feel something like that. I remember burying my dead dog, Princess, when I was younger. I mean, I watched my brother do it. They told me that our neighbour poisoned her. I don't doubt it. I had nightmares for weeks after that. I dreamt that Princess was calling for me. I told my parents that they buried her alive. Of course they didn't but I truly believed that they did.

I don't think I want to be buried. Coffins are expensive. I remember when they buried my grandmother they bargained to lower the cost in front of her corpse. I wonder if she was there listening. It was pretty coffin though. It was lined with blue velvet and it looked comfortable. It was white and adorned with daisies and there was a window where I could see her face. I didn't look for long because she didn't look like herself.

I don't think being cremated would be any better. You are skin and bone one second and then ashes the next. Do I want to sit on your shelf in an urn forever, forgotten and treated like furniture, clashing with your décor so you consider putting me away but you feel guilty so you keep me there, but over the years you grow to hate my urn? You grow to hate me. I know people throw ashes into rivers but my uncle still has my grandfather's ashes with him. It has been three years since his death. I think my uncle forgot that he even has them. Someday those I know will forget about me. They will forget my face and eventually they will forget my name. I know because I can't remember the faces of those who have left me. I only have their names and some memories that are slowly fading. I wonder what happens when everyone forgets about you. It would be like you never existed.

Maybe I will be remembered if I haunt everyone when I am gone. I don't know how hauntings work though. How does one decide to stay? Would I even want to stay when I could go anywhere I please? I know I would haunt my sister because I know she will take my clothes. She would probably wear one of my dresses to my funeral. What would I wear to my funeral? If it will be up to her she will choose something she doesn't like. I hope they choose something black. How do I let them know these things? How do the dead let anyone know anything? Do they just stand by and watch their sister choose that ugly pink dress they once wore to a wedding? I felt pretty when I wore that dress so I won't mind. I think haunting people in a pink dress would be disturbing. I wouldn't mind being remembered that way.

I hope they say nice things about me at my funeral. I have never attended a funeral where anyone was happy to see their loved ones go. I hope they say that I changed their lives. I don't think I did but it would be nice if they said it. I hope they exaggerate all the things I've done because I've lived a dull life thus far. I wonder if anyone has ever lied when standing at the pulpit, looking down at a coffin with hundreds of eyes on them. Would there be hundreds of eyes at my funeral? Do I know that many people?

I have heard elderly people say that they hope that they die in their sleep. I can't decide if bleeding out is a bad way to go. It is slow but it isn't unpleasant. My blood is cold now and it feels sticky so it's uncomfortable but as long as I don't move, it isn't too bad. I don't think dying in your sleep is a good way to go at all because though it may be quick, there is no time to remember all the memories.

I wouldn't mind suffering a little more if I can keep my memories just a little longer. I could linger on them and that is what death could be, just never waking up from the best memories.

I feel colder now and the pain is fading. I tuck my hands underneath me and I notice that my body doesn't hurt too much anymore. My toes are stiff. So is the rest of me. It is just cold now. I reach for my blanket and throw it on me. I feel a slight cramp in my stomach but I just close my eyes. It is just another day in May after all. Another day of bleeding and cramps and crying for no reason. I will bleed today and tomorrow and the day after. Then it all goes away till June. It comes around again in July, then August. I will bleed each month till one day I won't. Till then I will contemplate death as I bleed out.

THIS IS A SHORT STORY

This is a short story. It is a story of something not being where it is supposed to be. It's not because I misplaced it. I'm used to misplacing things but I swear that this time I didn't lose it. It was just there one day and then it wasn't.

I felt her inside me before I even saw her on the doctor's monitor. She looked like a speck of dust in the middle of a tornado. I couldn't even find her before the doctor pointed her out. When she did I couldn't believe that something so small could mean so much to me. I stared at the photo of the little speck all the way home.

I pinned the photo to my fridge with my favourite fairy magnet. It was a fairy with lilac wings that wore a lavender crown and I felt like it fitted the little speck. At that time I didn't know I was having a little girl. I didn't know for sure but I had an inkling. I had an inkling that inside me there was a caterpillar that would one day turn into something beautiful.

For her, I did everything I was told. I ate things that made me nauseated. I drank many different things that tasted like the colour green. It wasn't a pleasant green. They tasted like the mud I had once eaten on a dare. They tasted like a swamp filled with mud and the acai berries inside didn't make them taste any better. I stopped drinking coffee which was something I never thought would ever happen but I did it for fear that it would be bad for her. I was given glasses of different sizes with liquids of every colour but I didn't question anything. I just took what I was given no matter how it smelled or tasted because it was for her.

Knowing she was with me everywhere I went changed a lot of things. I had always been clumsy but with her I became cautious. I didn't take a step without being sure of my footing. I used to be annoyed at people who walked slowly on sidewalks but I became that person. I used the zebra crossing when I would usually dash across. I wore looser clothes in case I suffocated her. It was stupid but I was vigilant for the first time in my life.

I told her stories about my life. We, my husband and I, would talk to her for hours, though her ears probably weren't developed yet. We sang to her, albeit badly, so she would recognise us when she eventually met us. I told her about the places we would take her and about the pretty dresses I had gotten her. My husband would always intervene to tell me that boys don't wear dresses but I think he knew that she was a girl too.

I felt her at every moment of every day. She became the best part of me. I loved her and by extension I loved myself. I never loved myself before her. I never loved anything or anyone the way I loved that little speck. I gave her my best. I gave her everything I had: my mind, my body and my heart. That is why I don't understand what happened.

There was supposed to be a baby in me. A baby was supposed to be born but it wasn't. I felt the moment I lost her. Not because of the blood that ran down my legs. Not because of the sudden pain in my gut. I knew it when I didn't feel her anymore. She was there one moment listening to my bad singing and the next she was gone.

I don't know what I did wrong but I can't help but think that it's my fault that she isn't here. Everyone tells me that it isn't but there must have been something more I could have done. I was supposed to protect her. I failed. I lost her.

I had already picked out a name for her. I told my husband that he could choose the name if the baby was a boy but I knew she was a girl. My little speck would have been named Lila for the lilac on the fairy wings that she reminded me of. I dreamt about teaching her how to say her name and about showing her that lilac fairy. I dreamt of teaching her to write it down on her notebooks before I took her to school someday. Instead, all I have is her name inscribed on a gravestone next to a statue of a little fairy.

I told you this was a short story. It was barely a sentence. Her story ended before it even began. It's been six years since the day I lost her. I am reminded every day of her when I look at my four-year-old. She wears Lila's dresses and plays with Lila's toys and I think of how they would have played together. I see her in everything. I sometimes wonder if she knew how much I loved her. I hope I showed her in that hundred days she was with me how much she meant to me. I see the fairy magnet that still holds up the only picture of her that I will ever have and I hope that somewhere up there, there is a little fairy named Lila with lilac wings waiting for me.

SHE UNRAVELS

She picks a spool of thread. She doesn't care what colour. She unravels it and threads a needle with ease. She then chooses the fabric from the many options that hang on her walls. She chooses one that matches the colour of the thread. She knows the measurements by heart as she cuts the brown tracing paper. She cuts out the body piece then the sleeves, the skirt and the collar piece. She attaches the paper to the fabric and cuts. All she hears are the snips of the blade, sometimes accompanied by the satisfying rip of fabric. She cuts a perfect line every time.

They expect a few garments from her at the end of every day. She is used to meeting their expectations. They pay her a pittance for her work, barely enough for her family to live on. She sits on her bed as she sews in the middle of a large room surrounded by walls of fabric covering the deteriorating wooden walls. She smells the decay no matter where she sits. The smell is gradually replaced by something else. She could never put her finger on it. It smelled of familiarity and comfort. She looks down at her needle and smiles. The fabric is stained red, though it looks brown today because the fabric is blue. The scent calms her and she sews till she is finished. She soaks the garment in warm water and the blood washes away. She hangs it on the clothing line that runs from one end of the room to the other.

Then she picks another spool of thread, the colour doesn't matter. It never has and it never will. She cuts the fabric and it all starts again. This time she makes a skirt. She doesn't look down. She knows that every seam she creates is right. It feels right. She hears the whispers of her blood and they tell her she is right. She delights in the pain she feels as the needle's point sinks into her skin. It's the only time she ever feels anything at all.

She gets lost in the stitches, her mind buried in the seams. She has to get this done. She has to work faster. She has to use up all the fabric. She tries to but there is always more. She has never seen the wooden walls she smells decaying. All she sees is cloth. All she sees are colours. There is always more.

Her fingers are mangled and sticky now. The needle drips with blood. The thread is dyed a bright burgundy. She doesn't remember what colour it was before. The thread sticks to her fingers. As she tries to pull the thread away, her skin comes away too. She stops to wash her hands and then she continues. She is blood and thread.

They find her usual stack of clothes ready for sale, not a seam out of place. They also find her lost in her blood. They bandage her hands and give her a thimble. They tell her they expect the same stack tomorrow.

She wakes up the next morning, puts the thimble on and gets to work. Her bleeding thumbs are no more. She is still surrounded by walls of fabric. It is all she sees. It is all she is. She threads her needle with ease and she cuts the fabric. She lets the scissors go where they please, taking bits of her skin off too. She has to get this done. She has to work faster. She has to use up all the fabric. She doesn't understand that there will always be more. She will never see the wooden walls. She will be surrounded by cloth and spools of thread all her life. All she has is thread as she sews away the rest of her days.

Today they bring her a sewing machine. She has never seen one before. She has never even heard of them before. She has heard nothing for a long while actually. She has seen nothing but cloth and thread. After teaching her how to use the machine, they tell her that they expect more clothes tomorrow or her wages will be deducted. She doesn't make much but it is better than nothing. A wage cut would mean that one of her children will starve. She threads a new needle and gets to work.

She sits at the sewing machine, her new companion, and as she sews, she lets her mind roam free. Alas, her mind doesn't know what freedom is. It stays focused on the walls before her. Red, blue, green, orange, purple. Rainbows before her and behind her. They are everywhere she looks. They are everything she touches. She longs for grey and shades of black but those do not sell in this town.

She doesn't know if she likes the machine. Her hands worked faster. She was more familiar with every inch of a needle than the many nooks of a sewing machine. She has no time to get used to it because there is a knock at the door. She folds her last garment and puts it in a pile. Someone walks in and carries the garments away. For a second she has nothing to do. That second never lasts. She cannot rest or her children will starve.

She picks a spool of thread. It doesn't matter what colour. Nothing ever matters. She unravels it and threads the needle. She then chooses the fabric from the many options that hang on her walls. She chooses one that matches the colour of the thread. She knows the measurements by heart as she cuts the brown tracing paper. She cuts out the body piece then the sleeves, the skirt and the collar piece. She attaches the paper to the fabric and cuts. All she hears are the snips of the blade as it slides through the fabric. She cuts a perfect line every time. Thus her life goes on and on. Snip after snip, loop after loop. A never-ending cycle of thread and cloth.

THE CURSE OF AN EMPTY NEST

I used to wake up each morning to our roosters crowing. Their cries, each one unique in their shrillness, greeted me each day in their cacophonous chorus. They never crowed at sunrise though. They somehow only crowed in the late morning when they were hungry. They didn't make for reliable alarm clocks.

The chickens lived in a makeshift coop that my father fashioned out of metal wires and decaying wood that he had found in a junkyard. It wasn't the sturdiest of fixtures but it worked for us. Each morning before I was old enough for school I would stumble out the door, barely awake, to the coop with a bucket of chicken feed. It was a heavy bucket filled with leftovers, worms, and barley grains. At the sound of the rusted hinges of our front door creaking, I would be surrounded by the chickens in an instant. The roosters would rush out first, followed by the hens, clucking and pecking at each other to reach me first. As they would crowd around me I spun around with the bucket, throwing its contents in the air. The chickens would begin pecking the dirt long before the food hit the ground. They were not very bright.

I was also in charge of collecting their eggs. I could always tell when there were eggs ready to collect. The hens would screech all day and when the screeching died down, there would be nests full of eggs. I looked forward to those days. The atmosphere in the dingy coop changed from morbidly depressing to somewhat pleasant. The hens would welcome me with excited clucking, which was a lot like their usual clucking, only even more incoherent. I would have a treat ready for all of them. It was usually sunflower seeds. As I reached out to collect eggs with one hand, I offered them seeds with the other. That way they didn't notice as I collected the eggs. They merely continued on, snacking on seeds and clucking away. It was during that period that my fingers were pecked the least. They even let me pet them. That's how I knew that they were happy.

After I collected the eggs, I would arrange them in a cardboard box filled with hay and carry the box to my mother. She would examine each one and tell me what a good job I had done. I liked hearing that. It was a nice change from being ignored by her. She would crack one of the eggs into a wok spitting with oil and as the egg began to cook, she would throw a handful of rice in. She seasoned it with many spices. I still can't name them all. It was a rare treat that she only gave me when there were at least three dozen eggs. She also saved a couple of eggs to make my father a bhurji[7], his favourite breakfast. He usually had it with a paratha[8]. He used to feed some to me when my mother wasn't near. It was delicious. The rest of the eggs were sold at the market. They would disappear as soon as my mother set them out.

I spent most of my day talking to the chickens. I like to

____

7   Indian scrambled eggs with spices
8   Unleavened flatbread

think that they understood me but they probably thought I was clucking in a language they didn't understand. Maybe they merely entertained me because they knew I would have seeds for them as a reward for listening to my ramblings. Perhaps they thought of me as a friend or maybe they didn't think at all. I didn't mind that they didn't answer me. All that mattered was that they listened. It was more attention than I had from anyone else in my life when I was young.

Looking after the chickens was no Herculean task but it wasn't easy. It wasn't easy because we didn't have a gate to keep the chickens from wandering into the street. It was an open neighbourhood, so no one had one. Some nights when I would hear the sound of squawking chickens, I would wake up hopeful that it was an egg. It wasn't always an egg. Sometimes it was roadkill. A chicken or two would wander out of the coop and into the street. They screeched as they got crushed under the wheels of lorries that drove past. I would cry for days, mourning the loss of my friends. I like to think that the other chickens mourned their friends too but I don't think they cared. My parents would tell me that they would replace the dead chicken and they did but it wasn't the same, at least for me.

Another thing that made looking after the chickens difficult was when one of them didn't lay eggs for a while. The first time I told my father, he told me to give the hen a few more days. When she still didn't lay eggs after a month, he went into the coop and broke her neck. After that I tried to hide the lack of eggs from some hens from him but my mother would notice the inconsistent number of eggs and tell him. He would go into the coop to collect eggs and come out with a carcass. As much as I cried each time he did that, he continued to do it. He tried to explain to me that a hen that laid no eggs was of no use. I told him that maybe she could help some other way. He told me that her only use was to lay eggs. If she couldn't do that, then she was just taking up space. The funny thing was he let the old roosters die a natural death though they were of no use. Somehow it felt like the other chickens felt the same. They didn't mope or cluck like they usually did when their egg-laying comrades passed on. No one mourned the barren dead chickens but me.

That last memory crosses my mind every once in a while, especially today as I sit in a clinic with my legs spread, waiting for someone to tell me that I am not the problem. They insert what looks like a giant needle with a hook on its end up between my legs and they warn me not to move. They tell me to hold my breath as they go deeper and I try not to make a sound as they scrape my walls and collect samples. Fear has prompted me to rush to the clinic as just this morning news of an old classmate's death had reached me. They say she was beaten to death by her husband as she couldn't produce a child. He isn't going to be put on trial for murder as everyone thinks it is justified. She hadn't carried out her duty, they say. No one mourns her, not even her family. They say that she was an embarrassment to her husband and say, 'Good riddance!' because now that she is gone he can marry someone who can give him an heir. I had rushed to the clinic to get checked as it was my husband who told me what had happened. It sounded like a threat coming from him.

It has only been about half a year since I sat on a dais

and he tied a thali[9] around my neck but ever since our wedding day, the question from all our relatives has been, 'When are you having a baby?'

My husband is desperate to answer the question with news of my pregnancy. Each night since the day we entered our new home, I am forced onto our bed and held down as he does as he pleased. As he holds me down I close my eyes and try to stay as still as I can though I want to kick him off me. When he is done he asks me to move aside so he can sleep. It hurts to move but I don't want him to touch me so I roll to the side and give him space. I lie on my side of the bed, holding back tears as I wait for the pain, the intense burning, to disappear. It usually does but the soreness remains. I asked him once if we could hold off for one night so I could recover from the soreness but he ignored me as he pinned me down. It felt as if sandpaper was being scraped against an open wound and I think I bled a little. I told my mother about what was happening but she told me that it is normal. She said it would stop when I give him a child. I asked her how to do that but she didn't have an answer. She told me to just lie there as he knows what to do.

Each month when I continue to menstruate, he grows more despondent. I didn't think anything could possibly be wrong as it would only be a matter of time before I would get pregnant. That is how it is for all the married women I know. They get married and then there is a baby. If she is fortunate it is be a boy. If not, she tries till she gets a son. My mother couldn't do that because after she gave birth to me there were complications. I was told that story

---

9 A gold chain worn by Indian brides to signify marriage

many times when I was young. She told me how I had ruined her. Each time I messed up she would say, 'This is why I wanted a son'. I think she still holds it against me.

I don't think I would complain if I had a girl. At least it would be a baby and this torture would end or at least halt till I have to do it all again to get a boy. It wasn't until I heard of women who couldn't produce eggs that I began to fear that I may be one of them. I was afraid that the longer I didn't get pregnant, the more likely it was that he would break my neck. Hearing about my old classmate's fate only increased my trepidation.

Now, sitting on a leather cushioned tall table holding back tears, I can only wait for my verdict. I still feel the scraping of the needle against my insides. The soreness is easy to bear as I am used to it now. When the doctor comes out holding a file, I try to read her face to see if she will give me good news. She gives nothing away. She takes a seat at her desk and tells me to join her. I stand up and quickly hold on to the table for support as my legs give out. When I am sure that I won't fall over, I head to the seat the doctor had gestured to. She opens my file and she tells me that there is scarring on the outer tissue of my privates.

'Is that something I should be worried about?' I ask and she repeats my question back to me. I shake my head. Surely the scarring must be normal. My mother had said that feeling sore was only expected. It was confirmed by other women who had offered me unsolicited advice on how to get pregnant. Most of the advice consisted of staying still and not moving too much after.

The doctor discusses other things like consent and infections, things that probably matter to someone else but though I try to care, I can't focus on any of it. I only came for one answer and she saves that for last.

'Can I have a baby?' I ask and she smiles.

'There is nothing stopping you from that. Everything looks good. It is only a matter of time.'

I head home more relieved than happy to know that I have eggs. They just haven't been laid or fertilised, as she said.

More time goes by and by then the neighbours join the discourse on what is going on between my legs. It's not right for a woman to not have children, they tell me. I tell them that sooner or later it will happen. It doesn't stop them from giving me pitying looks. My mother and mother-in-law begin to visit too, bringing herbs to make concoctions for fertility. No matter how many times I remind them of what the doctor had said, they tell me that there has to be something wrong with me.

My husband's despondence shifts to bouts of rage. Each night he practically throws me aside when he is done. There is no more talking, only yelling. I start wearing saree blouses with longer sleeves to hide the blue-black swelling that forms on my arms where he grabs me. I don't think any of the villagers would care even if they saw it. They begin gossiping about me so the sight of bruises would only add fuel to fire. I can almost picture what they would say. They would say it was justified as I couldn't carry out my only role as a wife. They would call me a barren chicken and say that my time was running out. I fear that it is. I fear that my husband's bouts of rage will end with my broken neck.

I rush back to the clinic again to tell the doctor that she was wrong. I tell her to do the test again. Though she tells me that I am fine, I beg her for any medicine to help me get pregnant. She tells me that she has nothing to help as there is nothing to fix.

'You are not the problem,' she tells me but I tell her that I must be since there is no baby in me. She tells me that it is not my fault. I find it hard to see how that could be. She hands me a pamphlet and tells me to read it. As I head home with the knowledge that nothing is wrong with me, I peruse through the trifold pamphlet and suddenly I understand what the doctor was telling me. I am not the problem. He is.

Though I came to the realisation, I don't know what to do about it. I know that the moment I bring it up he will become hostile. Well, more hostile than he already is. He has already begun to call me an embarrassment and a curse. He tells me that women like me were punished with empty wombs for things that we had done in the past. He calls me a cheap whore and tells me to repent. He isn't the only one to call me names. The gossiping has reached new heights. My mother arrives only to tell me that the villagers have told her that I am cursed. She has come with more herbs to help remove the curse. She makes tons of herbal blends but nothing she does fixes the problem.

When I tell her what the doctor had said and show her the pamphlet, I don't expect the slap that she gives me.

'This is all your fault. How can you blame your husband? He looks after you and you cannot even give him a child. He should kill you for even thinking like this.'

I remember the carcass my father threw out after he broke the neck of yet another hen. He did it at my mother's prompting. I'm not surprised that she thinks I deserve the same fate. I wouldn't be surprised if she is the one who pulls the trigger.

As the gossiping worsens, so does my husband's temper. He now insists on starting earlier in bed so we can try more. Each time he grabs me I am tempted to tell him that he is the problem. His hold on me stops me from saying anything. I don't want to feel that pressure around my neck. I know he will snap it easily then throw me off the bed and go to sleep. I keep telling myself that broken roosters don't get broken necks, only barren hens do and it is easier to stay silent than cluck and be punished.

Silence is the only solution I have for now. It is a Band-Aid over a festering wound. I can tell that my days are numbered. I feel it each time I bleed for the month. One day his patience will run out. One day he will walk into our room and break my neck and no one will mourn the barren dead chicken. I now look forward to that day.

THE PARADOX OF PORCELAIN HEARTS

The paradox of porcelain hearts stems from a shattered heart. It is a cycle of damage that occurs when a shattered heart attempts to be whole again. This restoration requires the sacrifice of other hearts. It begins with a whole and intricately painted porcelain heart that tells the story of someone who has hope. Each heart is unique. She decorated hers with leaves and vines that sprouted sweet peas occasionally. Each brushstroke was made with love and with each blooming sweet pea, that love grew. Her porcelain heart beat in rhythm with the wind, like wind chimes twinkling as the pipes patter the porcelain. It played a beautiful melody for the world to hear. It was a thriving heart but that was a long time ago. She didn't stand a chance because lonely people break beautiful hearts and hers was the loveliest anyone ever saw.

With a heart like that she had wanted to help the world so she cracked her heart whenever anyone asked for a piece. She gave away pieces even when no one asked for them. She fixed problems that weren't her own and let other people's problems occupy her thoughts. She was an outlet for the feelings of others while her heart suffered. She chipped away at her porcelain heart so that those around her could heal. For a while, seeing others smile brought her happiness. They loved her and she loved them for it was the only thing she knew how to do. With her love came sacrifice. She gave them everything and they were happy. What she didn't realise was that people are addicted to happiness. They ravaged her heart and took their fill and then some because happiness was scarce and hers was in abundance.

Some called her naïve, others said she was too trusting. Whatever she was, she grew out of it. She learned that a cracked porcelain heart dropped pieces more easily. She learned that those around her wouldn't hesitate to take the fallen fragments. The day came when they stopped asking. They just took what they wanted and thought she wouldn't mind. She was generous. Little by little, she fell apart and they picked up the pieces and left. She asked those she helped for some fragments of her heart back but they were strangers now that they had taken what they wanted from her. Her heart fragments were now theirs. The fuller they got, the emptier she became.

Her peace of mind was the first to go. She grew wary of those she once trusted with her life. She couldn't trust them not to hurt her. She couldn't trust anyone anymore. The girl who once laughed freely, shrunk into herself as her heart slowly disappeared. The hollow feeling in her chest tasted bitter and that is what she became. She had lost her happiness and with it, she lost who she was. Her vines wilted away and sweet peas had no chance to grow let alone bloom. In the place of her once beautiful heart was a fragment, just a minute fraction of what it once was.

The last thing to go was hope. She lost it when those she had helped didn't do the same for her. She knew that no one owed her anything but she had hoped that maybe someone would help. When they let her down, she broke. With hope gone, though she clung on to the last fragment of her porcelain heart with all her might, she had no fight left in her. So they took that from her too. What she did cling on to was the bitterness and the ugliness they left in their wake. She didn't need hope. Hope and love had led her astray so she left them behind.

Her life, void of hope and love, was one filled with anguish and hatred. Fear was at the base of it all. She lived in fear of being hurt again and that made her push people away. She was cautious with every bit of happiness she managed to gain and she was greedy for more. No one liked her anymore and she knew why. It was because she didn't have anything they wanted. They didn't like what she had become because it didn't benefit them. Mostly they didn't like her because she stopped caring about what they thought about her. She had realised that they thrived off her need to be loved by all. They had cured her of that. The tragedy of it all was that she stopped caring, but to her it was a victory.

This is where the cycle ends and a new one begins. A soul with no hope and love is a lonely one. And lonely people break beautiful hearts. That is exactly what she did. She didn't live to please any more. She took and took from those naïve enough to give her a chance. She envied their happiness and her taste for it could not be satiated no matter how much she took. She understood why they took the pieces of her heart when she once offered it to them. She would have done the same. Learning from what they did to her, she continued the cycle and destroyed everyone she met. She stole fragments of their porcelain hearts and left them broken. She had no remorse. It is what they did to her after all.

Little by little her heart began to grow again. It didn't look the same, made up of mismatched fragments, but how could it when it came from a dark and lonely place? Made up of the pain of others, how could it be anything but ugly? What once sounded like wind chimes was now a clanging bell and sadly she couldn't tell the difference, or maybe she could but she didn't care. With each piece she collected she got a taste of the happiness she once had. She searched for that high but what she hadn't learned was that no amount of happiness that she stole would ever make her whole again. She would never taste the happiness she once had. She might have gotten echoes of it in the fragments that she stole, but it would never be the same. No one is ever the same.

That is the paradox of porcelain hearts.

LOUD MINDS AND QUIET PEOPLE

~

I remember a time when I had a quieter mind. It hasn't been quiet for a while now. Today, like every other day, it tells me the many ways that things could go wrong. It also tells me what the probability is that I will be the reason for things going awry. In a household made up of sons, and mothers who dote on them, I will always be wrong. It is something I have gotten used to. I live in anticipation—no—trepidation of someone yelling my name. It is exhausting living with a constantly racing heart and cold hands but I can't blame my body for the state of my mind. I can only blame myself.

Ever since I was young I have taken each day like a series of battles I must fight in order to get through the day. The moment I walk out of my room, it begins. The daily warfare starts with my mother.

'Why are you like this? How can you wear that when you have brothers? I can see your nipples. Go and change.'

I remember asking her years ago why I should change. The scar running across my palm from the rattan rod she struck me with in reply reminds me to never ask again. After years of the same comments about my clothes, you'd think I would have learned. I guess my mind didn't prepare me for everything then. I go back to my room and put on a bra before she can start yelling.

I used to anticipate things going wrong at breakfast but I couldn't skip it because that would have caused problems too. My mother had the habit of forgetting that I eat breakfast. Sometimes my brothers forget too. Once, I decided that I would be the first one at the table. I wanted to know what a full stomach felt like. I left my room the moment I heard my mother in the kitchen. I was prepared to start eating before my brothers were even up. The smell of thosai[10] and dhal curry was already wafting through the house. I rushed to the table and took a seat. My mother was at the stove pouring the thosai batter onto a flat iron slab. She turned around when she heard the chair creak.

'Can I have two?' I asked and she looked surprised.

'You can't eat before your brothers. Go and wake them up,' she said.

'Why? Can't they eat later?'

'Don't ask stupid questions. Just do what I say,' she said.

The moment they got to the table, she started serving them. She gave them four thosai each. I gave her my plate like they did but she said, 'Am I your servant? Go and get it.'

I went to the stove but there was nothing made. Only the batter was there. I poured it onto the slab and waited till it was done. I flipped it onto my plate and poured some curry on it. There wasn't much curry left so I made sure not to take too much.

'Can I have that?' my brother asked the moment I sat down.

I told him no but he looked to my mother.

'Give it to him. You can make more,' she said. When I

---

10 Crepe-like South Indian dish made of lentils and rice

didn't pass him my plate, she came to me and before picking the plate up, she added, 'Always making life difficult for everyone. Can't even share. How can a girl be selfish? Who raised you like that?'

I didn't feel offended because she had said that so many times before. Selfish, ungrateful, stupid. I don't know a time when she has called me anything else. She pinched me as she said, it like she always did, and I let her. She took my plate and passed it to my brother. He shovelled it down in about fifteen seconds and left the table to wash his hands. I got up to leave too but I was stopped by my mother.

'Who is going to wash your plate?' she said.

I wanted to ask her why my brothers didn't have to wash their plates but I remembered the last time I asked. She had slapped me and said, 'You are a girl. Learn to do housework. Don't be lazy.'

Since I didn't want to be slapped again, I took my plate and went to the sink. She stopped me again.

'Take the other plates also,' she said. I did as she demanded. I learned early on that talking back to her wasn't worth it. She would have complained to my father and told him that I was being disrespectful and then I would get in trouble with my father too. She taught me to respect the men in my life and do anything I could to please them. I don't know why she went out of her way to do so much for them and do nothing for me. I only know that she expected me to do the same.

After washing the plates, I went back to my room. I was hungry but I got used to it over time. Home was a place that I felt suffocated in so I spent more time in school. That was until that was taken from me too.

I attended a co-ed school. I wasn't the best student because I wasn't really interested in anything. The one thing that made me excited to go to school was basketball. I played basketball for the school's girls' team. During one of our practice sessions, we were told to join the boys' team. I never really had any problems with any of the boys like my friends did because the boys knew my brothers. It was the only thing that kept them away. At least it did for a while.

During that practice, I learned that I would always be wrong no matter what. One of the boys pinched my thigh as I walked by. I went to our coach and reported to her what had happened. I expected her to tell him off.

'Pull your shorts lower so they can't see your thighs,' she said. My friends were told the same thing. When one of the boys grabbed a girl's breast, it was announced during our morning assembly that girls would be required to wear a t-shirt two sizes larger so as to not be a distraction. Shorts were also not allowed. I went home and complained to my parents about it. 'What do you expect when you show everything? I told you not to wear shorts,' my mother had said.

I quit basketball after that. I don't know what I expected from her but she always found a way to let me down.

With nothing to do but study, that is what I did. It didn't get me anywhere though. My mother made sure of that. I found out just recently, a few years after she died, how she hid my university acceptance letter. I know why she did it. She had a wedding match ready and she knew I would only say yes if I didn't get in. I wonder if she knew what that did to me. I needed that acceptance letter. I needed to know that I wasn't useless. I needed validation that I was good at something. Her hiding it from me made me doubt everything I did. I second-guessed myself at every turn. I kept quiet when I would usually speak because I wasn't sure if my words would make sense. She took my voice and my life. She ruined me and I hate her for it.

She prepared me well for my mother-in-law. That woman loves her son and sees me as the enemy. I don't know a polite way to tell her that I don't want her son because all he does is echo her words. She is good at telling me what to do. She is especially adept at telling me how everything I do is wrong. She tells me that the way I clean is lazy. She calls me stupid when I ask her questions she doesn't know the answer to. She calls me selfish when I sit by myself in the living room reading a book and she calls me ungrateful for not doing more for my husband. It is like having another mother. I feel quite at home with her.

She visits often and when she does she gives me advice that I never ask for. Once, she told me that I couldn't be seated at the table until my husband was done eating. She said it was more efficient to serve him that way. She told me she learned from experience. I remember my mother doing the same. She too would linger as my father ate. I started doing it too so I wouldn't disrespect my mother-in-law but when I tried to stop, my husband looked at me like I was vile so it became part of my routine too. I have changed many things because of her because I didn't like her disapproval. I began to wash the clothes by hand because she said that washing machines were lazy. I stopped buying new clothes because she told me I shouldn't use any money for myself because I didn't earn it. She tells me what to cook and how to clean. She sounds just like my mother and I think I hate her like I did my mother.

I want to tell her that I don't need her help but the voice in my head stops me. I haven't been able to stand up to anyone in forever so I know that it is just wishful thinking believing that I will ever have the guts to tell her to leave me alone. Even in my head I lose every battle because I can't seem to fight for fear of being disrespectful to those who do not hesitate to disrespect me.

I remember a time when the voice in my head was on my side. She told me to fight at every turn. Those days are long gone. She doesn't even sound like me anymore. She definitely isn't on my side. She used to like me, but she has grown to hate the way I can't get things right. She tells me to doubt myself and puts me down when I try to lift myself up. She tells me to keep quiet and to obey the people around me. She tells me I am selfish, ungrateful and stupid. The voice in my head telling me these things sounds familiar. I speak in the voice of my mother and I can't block her out no matter how hard I try. She suffocates me even from the grave.

I had thought I would be different from my mother. I had made sure to check myself when I was growing up each time I felt like I was becoming anything like her. She was the last person I wanted to be like but she is what I became.

Now I tell my daughter that she should wear longer shorts. I tell her to change her clothes because her nipples are showing. I prioritise my sons and teach them that women are lesser. I teach them that they should be served and I teach my daughter that she should serve. I make her second-guess herself and I put her down when she tries to speak. She used to be loud like I was but I taught her to be quiet and now she is only loud in her head. I don't know if what I am doing is right but I don't know another way. If I steer off the known path, I will make mistakes. I have been wrong too many times already. I can't risk it. I just want to feel that I am right for once. I just want to feel alright for once but I don't think I ever will, not with my mother in my head.

ODE TO SAREES

It is the cradle of a newborn, hung from a low beam, rocking back and forth as she slumbers. It gives comfort to the sleeping child because it smells like safety, like jasmine buds and incense. It smells a lot like her mother. The child sleeps for hours as the wind rocks her back and forth in her cradle of colours. When the child opens her eyes, though she is hungry, the bright motifs of filigree and florals distract her for a little longer until she cries.

Her mother hears her cries and pours cold milk into a charred pot. While waiting for it to boil, she chops green chilies and onions. She keeps a close eye on the pot though so it doesn't boil over. She has burnt milk many a time. As the milk begins to rise, she turns off the stove. She covers her hands with the pallu[11] of her saree and after making sure it is thick enough, she lifts the pot and pours the milk out into another one to cool it down. She repeats the process, pouring the milk from one pot into another until the steam is gone. Then she pours the milk into a bottle. The saree is her oven mitt.

Wiping her hands on her saree, she takes the milk to her child. The last time she didn't clean her hands, she had rubbed chili on the baby's face. She hadn't even realised

---

11 The end of a saree usually draped over a shoulder or over one's head

until she brushed her own hair out of her eye. It had stung and she quickly understood why the child was screaming. She soaked the end of her saree in water and wiped the child's face, leaving it bruised pink. Now as she goes to her child she wipes her hands on her saree again. The wind has taken on the task of rocking the child as it fusses in its makeshift cradle so the child isn't crying anymore. The saree is a cradle and a napkin.

More than a napkin, it is a towel. Her mother uses it to dry her child off after a bath. As she grows older, she creates uses for a saree of her own. After a meal, instead of washing her hands and mouth, the child runs to her mother and buries her face in her skirt. The skirt is already covered in oil and smells like spices as it is an apron too. Sometimes her mother smells like dirt because as she gardens, she rubs her hands on her skirt. The stains wash away easily so no saree is ever ruined.

The first time the child wears a saree, twelve years have passed. She is seated in the middle of the room as her coming of age is celebrated. She is fed black peas, porridge, raw egg and castor oil to strengthen and nourish her. She is given anklets and bracelets from all her relatives. The saree she wears is a symbol of her womanhood.

The girl, now a woman since she's bled, is allowed to wear sarees to auspicious events. She does so willingly. She likes the way people look at her. Be it weddings or festivals, she is dressed in her best. The saree only elevates her beauty.

With beauty comes boys and she has them lined up. She uses her saree as a ladder and climbs out her window almost every day to meet them. A saree is the perfect tool. Being eight metres long, it is the perfect length for her to reach the ground from her room.

She eventually does find someone she likes more than the rest and it isn't long until she puts on the most special saree of all. She had chosen the most expensive one on the shelf and they had gotten it for her without hesitation. As she walks to the dais, her anklets chiming with each step, she is a most beautiful bride.

Soon her sarees become cradles and napkins. Her child wipes their face on her and she lets them though she wants to push them away. She cooks and cleans and makes the same mistakes her mother did, wiping chili on her child's face and burning milk. She too cleans her messes with her pallu. She holds hot pots with it too. There is a new function for her saree though that her mother before her didn't experience. When her husband takes his jealousy, anger and spite out on her, her saree becomes a bandage. It soaks up blood and she begins to use it to hide her face as she leaves her house each day. No one is fooled but they do not do anything. It is between a husband and a wife, they say. She doesn't ask for help either. She knows no one would do anything. Instead, at night she uses her saree to wipe her tears. She wipes and wipes but there is always more.

The day comes when she puts on her last saree. She puts on her anklets and bracelets and picks one of her expensive sarees. She ties it onto the beam that held up her child's cradle and places a chair right below it. It is her child's cries that lead them to her. Her anklets chime as she hangs from a beam that once held her at a happier time. Filigree and floral motifs hold her up. She wears her last saree as she is burned.

What a magnificent invention a saree is. Eight metres

of cloth for a lifetime of adventures. Each fold is a story, a tragedy, a comedy, held together by tradition.

CREATING CONSTELLATIONS

If the stars are aligned just right, I could get hit by a bus. If an asteroid hits a ball of gas I could trip on nothing or fall off my bed. I could find treasure at the twinkle of a star or that same star could move an inch and cause an avalanche that would cause the roof over my head to collapse. That is all I hear when people read the stars and tell me that my fate lies in specks of dust light-years away. The sky is prettier at night with stars and I know they helped explorers thousands of years ago navigate, but to me they mean nothing. I don't think they were ever meant to mean anything, at least not important things like determining who you will spend the rest of your life with.

My marriage match was determined when I was born. Our birth signs that were determined by the stars were aligned and those who decided on the match said that a union like ours would mean maintaining the purity of my bloodline. It would also keep our wealth within the family. What romantic things to take into consideration. They wrote my name down next to a stranger's. He was only five years old at that time. I was of course unaware of any of the arrangements. It is not as if it concerned me or anything.

I understand why my mother never told me though. I had grown up pointing out the absurdity of our sacred traditions and practices and my mother stopped forcing me to take part in any prayers or festivals we had. I had pretended to care when I was younger but as I got older I didn't see the need to and my parents gave up trying to convince me that their beliefs meant something. It meant I didn't have to be up early picking flowers and suffocating from incense. I slept in as they sang their songs, spilled their milk, broke coconuts, and lit things on fire.

My parents never forced me to do anything. I was in charge of my life. I may have made bad decisions at times but they were at least my decisions and my parents were there to comfort me when things went wrong. It was nice knowing that they always had my back. They let me finish school, something many of my friends didn't have the luxury of doing. When I told them I would like to go to university, they didn't ask me what course I would be studying. They let me apply and paid my fees when I got in. They were there when I graduated and when I got my first job they celebrated by taking me shopping for new clothes. My mother told me that I had lucky stars but I don't think any of the things I did were written in the stars. I wrote my own stars and it worked for me. I knew I was fortunate that my parents let me do the things I did but that was as far as my luck went. I should have known though that all of it was a compromise. No one that enmeshed in incense and jasmine buds would ever be alright with me foregoing all their traditions. I can't believe I was naïve enough to think that they would let me get away. They expected me to repay their generosity and when they came to collect, I wasn't ready. You see they... Okay I think I started the story at the wrong place. I hate cliff-hangers but I'll have to leave you on a small one for a moment. We'll get back here later.

Anyway, I have a secret. My secret has a name. I don't think I should tell you his name because… because… well, you'll see why. We'll just call him Clark because he reminds me of Superman. I met Clark in university in my introduction to psychology class. I was taking it as an elective. He was too. He sat next to me in a room full of empty chairs and said hello. It was early in the morning and I wasn't in the mood to greet anyone so I just nodded in his direction. I opened my textbook and pretended to be engrossed in it hoping that he wouldn't want to start a conversation. He did. He asked what my name was and where I was from. I gave him monosyllabic replies but he didn't take the hint. He talked for about ten minutes and I don't remember half the things he said. It was a relief when class started. Alas, even that didn't deter him. He made observations and sarcastic remarks all through class and I made up my mind to not come to class early next time. That is until I saw his face.

At twenty-one I never had a chance to fall in love. I can't tell you what love feels like but I do know that my heart began to race and the moment he smiled as he said goodbye, I wanted to tell him to stay just a little while longer. Instead I told him, 'I'll see you tomorrow.' Though I tried, I couldn't stop smiling as I went home that day. I did see him the next day and all the days after that. We stayed back to go over what we learned for the day and we had lunch together after. Our meetings after psychology turned into meetings whenever we had free time after all our other classes. We studied together and when we weren't together we were texting and calling each other. I think it was the first time I found someone

I wanted to speak to. We would talk for hours and there was still so much to say the next day. Clark was like no one I had ever met before but I guess everyone says that when they are in love.

We met in many different places. There was a playground near my house and he would call me in the middle of the night. I would sneak out and meet him at the rusty swings. If I ever got caught it would have been the end of me and I was always paranoid that the creak of the swing would give me away. He made me a little less afraid when he took my hand. Sometimes I would go out on my bike and meet him at the end of the road leading out of town. It wasn't a long ride but I wanted to put as much distance between me and my parents as I could. I didn't know what would happen if they found out but somehow I knew that they wouldn't be happy. They may have been fine with the small things but I wouldn't get away with something like this. That is why most of our time was spent on campus. We stayed in the library and we booked study rooms just to talk and be with each other.

He knew me better than anyone I have ever met. He knew what was running through my mind and he was there to make sure I didn't get lost in my head. I was there for him too and we made each other better. He cured me of my scepticism while I made sure his head wasn't always in the clouds. We balanced each other out and I liked who I became. I didn't despise stars as much anymore and I even let my mother go on and on about them without snapping at her. He told me that I changed him too. He joked that he didn't know if it was for the better. I told him he was the best he had ever been. As we spoke, he took my hand. I intertwined our fingers and he began to smile.

'I love you,' he said. He caught me off guard but I didn't have to think long. I knew what to say.

Though I wanted to make a stupid joke or tease him I said, 'I love you too.' We tried to get back to studying but we couldn't stop smiling so we put our books away and continued talking. I don't think we said anything that made sense but we understood each other just fine.

In a town where there were no secrets, he was mine. Somehow no one knew about us all through our degree. I graduated at twenty-four and we got jobs at the same place. I will refrain from giving you too much information because it could get us in trouble. Being at work together we had even more time to spend with each other. We sat across from each other and discussed project designs and stayed late to meet deadlines. He always made sure to send me home. That is where we messed up.

My parents didn't find out our secret per se but they were suspicious. It's not appropriate for women to be out alone with men who aren't their husbands. It wouldn't bode well for their reputation and my parents cared a lot about reputation. That was part of the reason why they arranged my wedding without my knowledge. The other reason was because my time was up. I was at the perfect age to get married. People had begun asking and when my parents would usually ask me, they made decisions for me.

The moment they told me, I couldn't speak. It felt like everything around me was blurring into one.

'Who am I marrying?' I asked.

'It's your cousin. You have met him before when you were younger.'

'That's disgusting. I can't do that,' I told them. They seemed amused by my reaction.

'Your father and I are cousins,' my mother told me. When I didn't reply, they laughed.

'I won't marry him,' I said. Their faces fell when I said that and I regretted it immediately. I may have been loud when I didn't like things they made me do, but I had never disrespected them before.

'We have given you everything you have asked for. You have to do just this one thing for us. Can't you do that?' my father said.

I got on my own old bike and rode to the edge of town. I texted Clark and told him to meet me there. When he arrived he smiled and I didn't know what to do. He really did look like Clark Kent. I loved that smile. I loved that face. I loved him so much but I loved my parents more. Nothing I will ever do in my lifetime can repay my parents for the countless things they have given me when they had no duty to do so. They just gave and gave without asking for anything in return. I knew they were asking because it was our family reputation on the line. I may not have cared about that but they did. It's the one thing I could do for them. I couldn't change the stars this time.

'You wanted to see me?' he said. I nodded.

'I came to tell you that I am getting married.' He began to laugh but he stopped when I didn't join in.

'You can't,' he said, reaching for my hand.

'I have to,' I said. He asked me why.

'My parents are asking me to. They arranged my wedding when I was little. I said yes. I can't let them down.'

He didn't say anything. He just let go of my hand and walked back to his car. He drove off and I didn't try to stop him. I wouldn't even know what to say if I did. It was easy not believing in the universe when I made things happen for myself but it was hard to ignore the universe then.

I rode back home, tears running down my face and in the distance I saw his car. I pedalled faster and, throwing my bike aside, I rushed in. I will never forget the look on my father's face when he saw me. He looked disappointed.

'This young man says he loves you and wants to marry you,' he said. I heard the hurt in his voice and I knew what to do.

'I don't want to marry him. I will go ahead with the wedding you planned. Set the earliest date,' I said, not looking at either of them. Holding back tears, I headed to my room and that is where I let go. I cried till my eyes swelled and I hid my sobs in my pillow. When I woke up the next morning there were almost a hundred missed calls on my phone and a lot more messages from Clark. I didn't open any of them. I knew that if I read them I would change my mind. Instead I opened my laptop and sent an email, attaching my letter of resignation. I couldn't see him again.

My father acted right away and I was engaged just four days later. I hated every moment of it because everyone was happy but me. To make matters worse, I couldn't stop crying no matter how hard I tried. I kept quiet through it all though. I couldn't speak to my parents and they knew I didn't want to speak to them. I knew that they could see that I didn't want this though I told them that I did. I wanted them to call it all off but they didn't. They just carried on with all the rituals and traditions. They chose their reputation and their tradition over me and I chose them over myself like they knew I would.

The days leading up to my wedding would have been easier to bear if I could at least speak to Clark. He could always make me laugh even during my worst times. It wouldn't be fair to him if I called so I took respite in his messages. In each of them he begged me to meet him or to at least call him. He told me he loved me and that he wanted to marry me. I deleted those messages right away. I couldn't do that to my parents. I had to keep telling myself that or I would have let myself believe that there was a way out of this.

I knew the moment he heard about the wedding date. I was bombarded with more text messages and he called me at least a dozen times every half hour. He left me voice messages and I listened to them right away, desperate to hear his voice.

'You don't have to do this. They will understand. You told me they did everything they could so that you were happy. Why should this be any different?' he said.

Logic was never his strong suit but he made a lot of sense now. His persistence made me approach my parents to try one last time.

'I know I told you that I want to do this but I really don't,' I said.

There was no sympathy on my father's face. 'You will do as I say or you are no longer my daughter,' he said. My mother looked shocked but she said nothing.

I had never heard my father raise his voice in all my years so I knew that I was in the wrong. He didn't look like the same person who told me that I could do whatever I wanted. He looked hurt and I apologised to him and went up to my room. I played the voice messages over and over and reread each text. I wanted Clark now more than ever but I couldn't tell him. I knew that he would try to help but his help would have meant disappointing my parents.

That is something I would rather die than do.

Instead of trying anything more I decided to do nothing at all. I decided to let the stars determine what happened to me. It was not something I was used to but I found that it came easy to me. I woke up each morning and lay in bed all day. My mother brought me food sometimes and I took a nibble of it. I showered when I remembered to but I spent most of my time listening to his voice. It somehow made me feel hopeful that things wouldn't be so bad. I wished I took photos with him. I was always self-conscious about how I looked so I never did but now I wish I had. I missed his face, his laugh, how he made me feel, him. Now I would have to miss him the rest of my life but at least I had his voice telling me he loved me.

The days flew by with preparations for the wedding. I didn't get involved in any of it. My mother took my measurements and got me my saree. She dealt with my in-laws who I refused to meet. She made all the necessary arrangements so all I had to do was show up. I didn't even realise that it was my wedding day until she barged into my room with a whole group of people and told me to take a shower. She dressed me in my saree which I had never learned to tie by myself and the hairstylist, one of my many cousins, worked on my hair and makeup. I looked in the mirror and I didn't recognise myself. I looked thinner and sad, really sad, but I did look like a bride. I was halfway there. Now all I had to do was walk to the dais and take a seat. It would all go by quickly.

The bridal party accompanied me to the car. It was all so overwhelming because for months now I had been holed up in my room. The sun shone too bright and my cousins were too loud. I shook them off and got into the car by myself. As my mother helped me in she cupped my chin and forced me to look at her.

'I'm sorry,' she said.

I couldn't tell her that it was alright because it wasn't. She didn't wait for a reply. It could be because I hadn't said a word to her for months or it could be because she knew I would never forgive her or my father for this.

She got into the car and, along with a few of my cousins, we went to the temple. I didn't even recognise the place because I hadn't been there for years. I wondered if my new husband would force me to go. I knew that I would have to do as he asks or it would get back to my parents and their reputation would be ruined, much like my life. The temple was filled with people. Everyone my parents ever met was present. They were loud too. It made my head hurt so I pushed past them to get to the dais. I tried to spot the groom but I didn't even know what he looked like. I didn't bother to find out. He would be a stranger anyway.

As I made to walk to the dais, someone grabbed my arm. I turned around and there he was, the one person I wanted to see, Superman. Next to him were my parents.

'You need to leave now,' my father said.

'What do you mean?' I said. It was the first words I had said in months and my throat hurt from it.

'We shouldn't have made you do this. The only way to fix this is for you to run. We will say that you ran and that we will attempt to find you. You need to leave now,' my father said.

I couldn't understand what he was saying. There was no way my father would risk our family reputation like this.

'What about everyone here? They will say you brought me up badly,' I choked out.

'None of that matters. They can say what they want. The only thing that matters to us is you and your happiness,' my mother said.

'What made you change your mind?'

'You did. You could have run away or fussed and made things difficult for us but you stayed. You stayed because you respect us and love us and we were punishing you for it. We knew it was wrong from the start but you made us brave enough to do this,' my father said.

I opened my mouth to say more but only tears fell.

'You need to get her out of here,' my father said.

'How is he here?' I asked my parents.

'I told your parents about us and about how you didn't want to disappoint them. They gave me their permission to marry you,' Clark said. He was smiling my favourite smile and I couldn't help but smile too as more tears fell.

I turned to my parents and they were smiling. I hugged both of them before Clark took my hand that he had dropped forever ago and we ran. Well, we walked out of the temple to avoid any suspicion but the moment we were out, he pulled me along with him as he ran to his car. He took me to my house to pack and by the time the last of the guests arrived, we were long gone. I called my parents later that day and they laughed as they told me about all the chaos and panic. I apologised to them for disappointing them but they told me that that is one thing I could never do.

I guess my stars were aligned just right. I could have been hit by a bus, gotten crushed by an asteroid, tripped on nothing or fallen off my bed. Instead, the stars brought me Clark and just months after our getaway we got married. It was a small ceremony with his parents and mine.

There are still people looking for us so we are in hiding but I don't think they will ever find us. My parents are still carrying on the farce. Today, I am going to tell them that they are going to be grandparents. I know they will be happy. My mother will say I have lucky stars and I will agree with her.

THE MANY NUANCES OF SILENCE

There are many nuances of silence that pervade one's existence. She could tell the difference from a young age. She was born into a silent world after all. The only sounds in the room at the time of her birth were her cries. They echoed, hitting the ceiling and bouncing off the glass. They travelled through her clogged ear canals and hit her underdeveloped eardrums, playing a shrill and cacophonous melody. She didn't like the sound of it, nor was she impressed with the way it disturbed the silence, so she stopped. She didn't want to intrude. That was her introduction to the language of silence.

She was a quiet child. She learned to sit up, then crawl, then stand and fall, then waddle before learning to walk. Though she was taught how to talk, it wasn't something she enjoyed. She didn't like the sound of her voice nor did she enjoy the sound of anyone else's. The one sound she hated above all else was the sound of crying so, despite hating the sound of her voice, she used it instead of tears to get what she wanted. They began to call her a genius because she learned to speak faster than any other child could. She didn't care what a genius was, she just wanted silence. She taught herself not to cry and there was never a reason to because she had everything she could ever need.

She observed the world around her and picked up the

many types of silences there were and created silences of her own. There was her 'play pretend' silence where she would sit in a corner on linoleum flooring that resembled marble, and she would play with her toys. She wouldn't make a sound. It was all in her head. She had loud thoughts. She grew up loving toys that were silent, like her stuffed maroon teddy bear with a black bowtie and her collection of dolls. She put away anything that made a sound. Her squeaky duck was tucked under her bed where no one could step on it. She played with toys that had wheels only on her bed where the wheels wouldn't make that rumble they usually do when they slide across solid surfaces. She despised the toys that sang and those that spoke. There was a music box that she refused to wind up sitting at her side table while her wind chime never got a chance to twinkle. Her room was a silent sanctuary.

Another type of silence she learned of when she was young was the 'looking up at the moon' silence. Before bed, she would sit with her mother at her windowsill and, illuminated by the moon, they would sit in silent veneration of its beauty till one of them fell asleep. Her mother did most of the time. The girl would close her eyes and take in the silence that fell upon her as she felt her mother's heartbeat. She liked the silence of her mother and she didn't mind her sounds either. It was one of her favourite types of silences, the silence of a loved one.

She found intriguing silence in places no one bothered to explore. She learned of the 'watching ants march' kind of silence. She was intrigued by their rhythm and the inaudible patter of thousands of feet. When it had begun to rain once, she took out an umbrella and marched along with the ants until they reached their molehill. She didn't mind the sound of the rain because it brought with it another kind of silence, a melancholic and desolate kind of silence. She learned of the 'watching leaves fall' kind of silence and there was the 'wind brushing past leaves' kind of silence. She wondered where the wind was going and if it would ever stop. That too was a kind of silence, the silence of wonder. It was that kind of silence that filled most of her young days, along with the silence of curiosity and mischief.

When she was old enough to go to school, she learned of the silence that morning brought along with the sun. Every day as she woke up she would sit at the edge of her bed and close her eyes. It was a 'knowing you're alive' kind of silence and it excited her. It told her that today would be another day for silent adventures. It would be exciting time but also a tumultuous one because those around her lived a sonorous existence. They expressed joy by increasing their already deafening decibels and the girl was sure her eardrums would give up and walk out of her ears if she stayed around them for too long. She managed to find people like her who preferred finger painting to a game of whatever chasing each other while yelling was called. She added more types of silences to her encyclopedia. She added the silence of sitting on a see-saw and looking up at the sky as she flew high then descended and there was also the silence of swinging in a quiet playground as she waited for her mother to pick her up. She stopped playing on the swings after a while because its chains became rusted and began to creak. She believed that pain would sound a lot like that.

As she grew older, silence became more ubiquitous. No one she met wanted to talk much. They were caught up in their loud thoughts and in things they could not control. She was too. She was content with living in her head but there were moments where she would poke her head out and in one instance she found a new kind of silence. It was a silence that she had never encountered before. It was an 'I forgot how to speak' kind of silence coupled with an 'I think I forgot my name' kind of silence. It was a 'meeting a stranger's eyes in an empty classroom and knowing you wanted them in your life forever' kind of silence. That silence turned into an 'I've never seen such a beautiful smile' kind of silence and that spiralled into an 'I can't believe he's holding my hand' kind of silence. Before long it became an 'I can't believe he kissed me' kind of silence and they encountered many more beautiful nuances of silence that teenagers often found with their first love. She was stunned that he understood her silence and he was glad he met someone whose silence complemented his own. This silence had a name. It was Nate.

They started to meet under the twilight moon at a waterfall that flowed in the forest not far from her house. She snuck out each night through her window and he was there to catch her. Together they stumbled through the woods hand in hand in a silence that was theirs alone. They would sit on jagged granite at the edge of the waterfall and listen to cascades of water making their way to the bottom. The edges of her nightgown would be soaked as they lumbered back down what became a familiar path. He would kiss her goodnight before helping her climb back up into her room. She would sit at her windowsill and watch him slowly disappear just as the sun would rear its head. Hours later he would knock on her door and they would walk to school hand in hand, tired from their twilight adventures but happy that they had that twilight silence. It wasn't long before they encountered an 'I think I love you' kind of silence and they walked down that road together.

Though one part of her life was filled with enchanting silence, she couldn't immerse herself in it because her life at home had become filled with a disturbing kind of silence. This silence was deafening and though her mother told her to ignore it, as hard as she tried, this kind of silence didn't go away. It was a 'stand in the corner and watch your mother get beaten' kind of silence and after each painful, loud episode it was an 'ignore her bruises' kind of silence. Her mother cried silent tears and the girl found that she didn't like that silence because it was a 'do as I say or suffer' kind of silence. She now understood what torture sounded like. It was a leather belt on bare skin accompanied by a 'suppressed screams' kind of silence. She watched her mother flinch with every hit and all she could do was be silent.

She had believed long ago that what her parents had was a love that spoke through silence. They never acknowledged each other and she had believed that it was a different kind of love, one that didn't need words for others to know it was there. She wondered if she had missed something. She asked her mother and her mother told her that it was easier to hide things when the girl was younger because she didn't notice the world around her. Her need for silence had caused her to drown out the noise and live in the many nuances of silence that she had found. She apologised to her mother but her mother said, 'If silence was all you heard growing up then I did my job.'

She told Nate about it and he told her to never get

in the way because he knew what usually happened. He told her it would be best if she listened to her mother. She took his advice, mostly because it was what her mother begged her to do too. She didn't like it though. Each day she sat in her room and tried to reach for a silence that could drown out what was happening outside her door and she found that her loud thoughts combatted that of the whips. Little by little she formulated a plan. She didn't know what the end would be but she knew that whatever it was, it would be silent.

It started off as a plan to make her father suffer. She thought of how satisfying it would be for her mother if he could feel the leather belt break his skin. Her thoughts wandered to other weapons. She saw a rake in the front yard and imagined clawing at his back as he begs for her mother's forgiveness. *Knives are too easy*, she thought. She wanted to suffocate him as he slept and sometimes she prayed that the ceiling would cave in and kill him. The more she heard the whipping of the belt, the more her mind travelled. She was used to the quiet crevices of her mind and she willingly got lost in them. In her silence she planned things so horrifically beautiful. She wanted to break him like he broke her mother.

In the end she settled on a plan that would end her mother's suffering. Yes, breaking her father would do that but he would be alive and there was no guarantee that he would stop. He would be filled with more hate and he would eventually kill her mother. She decided that she would kill him first. It would be quick and more importantly, silent.

She worked on the plan alone. It wasn't a complicated plan. It only involved a rubber mallet and her mother's and hopefully Nate's cooperation. They could make or break the plan. She hadn't set the date to execute the plan but she knew that her father had to be stopped sooner rather than later.

The plan was set in motion the moment she hugged her father after dinner one night before excusing herself. She had loved that man once and that was her goodbye. She headed to her room and picked up the mallet. It wasn't heavy but it didn't have to be. Her rage would help. The sound of whipping that had begun spurred her on. She opened her door and walked down the stairs. No one heard her. She knew how to be silent. She sneaked up behind her father and as he pulled back the belt to swing again, she swung first.

She was never curious about what a mallet against a skull would sound like. She was surprised at how quiet it was. It was an eerie silence. *A dead silence*, she thought. She tried to hide her smile but she couldn't. As he lay there she couldn't help but think that the silence didn't suit him. He was loud and intrusive and he deserved an end that was just that. It wasn't part of the plan though so she let it go.

She went to her mother who was still crouched in the corner and offered her a hand.

'I have a plan,' she told her.

She asked her mother to get a bedsheet. Together they laid it out before lifting the body and placing it on the fabric. They wrapped the body up and kept it in the living room, his favourite room. She told her mother to wait for twilight. They cleaned the blood that had stained the linoleum flooring as they waited.

At twilight, the girl walked out the door and welcomed

Nate inside. He was on time as always. He looked confused but he followed her. She introduced him to her mother and then to her father. He flinched and asked her if she was alright. She nodded. He asked her what happened and when she told him what she did, he volunteers to take the blame. She told him he doesn't have to. None of them do. She admitted to both him and her mother that she had been planning this for weeks and that she knew what to do next.

They placed the body in the boot of the car and she gave her mother directions. She lead them into the woods, the sound of her heartbeat in her ears. They stopped at the entrance of the woods and, carrying the body, they make their way to the waterfall. They undid the knot on the bedsheet and pushed the body down into the darkness. She listened for the splash. They all did.

The walked out of the woods, filled with silence. She didn't know what kind of silence it was but she knew that it wasn't the silence of a guilty conscience. She felt her mother reach for her hand and when she turned to her, she saw her mother smile. The girl knew now what kind of silence it was. It sounded a lot like freedom and she liked the sound of that very much. She knew her mother did too.

As they got into the car, it started to rain but the rain didn't sound like desolation anymore. She told her mother to wash the bed sheet when they get home and they asked her how she knows that her plan will work. She told them that by throwing him down the waterfall, the impact from the head wound would look like her father fell down the waterfall and hit the rocks. She told her mother to make a missing person report in a day or two.

Twilight had waned and died by the time they reached

their house. Her mother headed inside and left her with Nate.

'I understand if you want to leave and never come back,' she told him.

'That would be a really weird thing to do to someone I love,' he said.

He leaned in and kissed her and she gave him her heart. They remembered that day as the day they discovered another kind of silence, the silence between hearts so in love that one would cease to beat without the other. It became her favourite kind of silence.

PROSPECT

*On knowing nothing
and everything*

THE VARIETY STORE

~

She picks up her fallen nose and dusts it off before sliding it on. It melted off in the sun again. The nose melds back into her skin seamlessly but she can feel it slowly droop. She adjusts it again and uses tape to keep it on. She had thought it looked flawless but since the new upgrade was announced, she had changed her mind. She regrets not getting the upgrade sooner. She is sure it will be sold out by now. Still, she rushes to the Variety Store where the bright lights on the signboard read: 'It has all you'll ever need.' The queue is long but it always is. She is used to it by now. All she knows is that it is always worth the wait. Perfection always is.

As the line shortens and she gets closer to the storefront, she catches a glimpse of the store display window. Bedazzled ribcages from last season are on sale. She had done away with hers and now donned the latest marble upgrade. It is heavier but she doesn't notice because the look on everyone's faces when they saw her had made it all worth it. It goes well with her translucent skin upgrade, an upgrade she had bought around the same time. She had been up to date with all the upgrades until two days ago when the nose upgrade was announced. They said it would be malleable, which would be helpful because it would give her more options to match it with her other accessories. She hopes they have one in stock. They always sell out on the first day. If she doesn't find one on the shelf she will have to beg her father to get one for her from the factory like she did with her diamond studded toenails. He understands that she needs to be up to date with the upgrades to be flawless.

She notices a girl in front of the store who looks almost her age. The girl stands out because she still wears her skin. No one does that anymore. *I wouldn't be caught dead in my skin*, she thinks, watching as the girl wanders away. She remembers when she was finally old enough to change. On her sixteenth birthday her parents gifted her a controlled acid wash. She had been dreaming of it ever since she saw her mother peel off her face and put on a diamond-encrusted filament over the pink dermis. She couldn't wait to do the same. The excruciating pain of acid over her skin had been easy to ignore because she knew it would only get better from there. In the red dermis that stared back at her she saw potential, the potential for perfection. Her brothers aren't as fortunate. They have to keep their skin all their lives. They would wrinkle and sag. She wouldn't. She would be perfect forever.

When she finally gets to the front of the line, she gets that familiar feeling in her chest. Her heart begins to race. Her palms prickle in anticipation. Everything she will ever need stares down at her, rows and rows of choices. The advertisement jingle plays in her head, '*All you'll ever need at your fingertips. The Variety Store is here for you*'. She anxiously waits to be let in. Somewhere in there is her new nose. She can feel it. She fiddles with her nose as she waits, lost in thoughts of upgrades and compliments.

She rushes forward the moment she is let in, pushing

past the other customers. They don't mind because they understand the excitement. The feeling never goes away, no matter how many upgrades they get. She all but runs to the section labelled 'Protuberance'. She sees jars of eyeballs, rows of fingers, and shelves of ears on the way, which tell her that she is close. Just around the corner she will see her nose. Her detachable heart thuds as she turns the corner. What she sees leaves her in awe. The wall of noses has that impact on everyone.

She looks up at the wall of never-ending noses hanging from hooks, ripe for the picking and she is ready. She knows what she is looking for and she won't stop until she gets it. She goes through the noses one by one, using a ladder to reach the topmost rows. She ignores the older upgrades. Those had not worked for her. Even if they had, they are out of style anyway and she couldn't bear the thought of wearing last season's nose on her face. The one she had on now was already causing her embarrassment and discomfort. She could feel the judgment in the eyes of everyone she spoke to. No, absolutely no other nose but the latest upgrade would do.

She spends hours looking, which isn't surprising considering the wall is almost twenty-five feet tall and almost as wide. She holds her mirror up to her face, gently picks up a nose and puts it back, repeating the action. None of them fit right but she knows that eventually, one will and so even though hours have passed, her determination doesn't waver. Anyone there for the first time would have settled for any nose but she knows the feeling of wearing the perfect nose and she chases that high.

The reward for her determination is the perfect nose. She spots it as she pushes the ladder toward the next row.

As she reaches for it, someone grabs it. Anger wells up in her chest and she yells, 'That's my nose!' The boy who had taken it starts a little, almost dropping the nose. She takes the nose from him and though he wants to argue, he is speechless. As she walks away, stunned at her own temper, he runs after her.

'You don't need that,' he says, blocking her path.

'And you do?' she says. He shakes his head.

'I mean the one you have on now looks great,' he says. She shrugs and walks away.

He doesn't know anything if he truly believes that, she thought. What is he even doing in here? Frazzled by the look in his eyes, she forgets to try on the nose. She rushes to the payment kiosk and after scanning the code on her wrist, she leaves. Instinct told her it was the right nose. She has to trust her gut this time.

She heads to the mechanics to get her nose installed. They would usually undo the screw of the old one and match the head of the nasal cavity to the new nose. She has gone through the procedure six times thus far, so she is familiar with it. On the way there she sees Malwares, women whose surgeries have gone wrong. They are all lined up outside a tent where they can get cheaper work done for them. She had learned from her father that those who couldn't afford the mechanics would go to those in the alleys to get fixed. She didn't believed it until now. She watches as the women wipe away blood that drips off their mangled faces. Some limp because of their broken hips while others have crooked limbs. She hears screams alongside the hum of drills coming from inside the tent. She quickens her pace.

When she finally reaches the mechanic shop, she is

relieved. Malwares are unpredictable. They want what she has and they will do anything to get it. Her father had warned her countless times that they would kill for parts. She scans her code and she is let in. She greets the woman at the counter and shows her the new nose. She is let through to the waiting area and inside she sees some of her friends. They are up to date with the upgrades too. It is what is expected.

She sees young girls in their original skin in the waiting room too. They look nervous. She wants to tell them that it will all get better after the acid wash but they will learn that soon enough. She hadn't met anyone who regretted getting rid of their skin. She hears screams from inside but she is used to it. They always scream but they come out with smiles on their new faces. Temporary pain is a small price to pay for beauty. When her name is called, she feels her heart race. She is one step closer to flawlessness again.

'Good luck,' someone calls. She ignores them. These things weren't dependent on luck.

She hands the nose to the mechanic and he leaves to find the right screw. He comes back with a tray of tools and she lies on the table. She closes her eyes and she feels him remove her last nose. He tugs at her nasal cavity and then it begins. She bites her cheeks to stop from scream-ing. *It is just temporary*, she tells herself. She thinks of how everyone will react to her and the pain disappears.

When she walks out of the room, she pulls out her mirror. She sees her nose and she is pleased. There is a ringing in her ear and she can taste blood but those things go away after a few hours. The throbbing in her head will take longer to heal but she is used to that too.

'I was wrong. This one looks better,' a voice says. The

boy from the Variety Store smiles at her.

'I didn't ask,' she says, though she feels pleased at the compliment. *Was he there the entire time? How did I not notice him?* She knows the answer. She was caught up in her new nose and who could blame her. He continues to walk alongside her, making observations from time to time but she ignores him. She expects him to leave but he stays by her side. He seems familiar but she doesn't know who he is.

'You'll be back there again soon,' he says, as she walks by the Variety Store on the way home. She nods. That's a fair assumption to make. Upgrades come out monthly, if not weekly. He continues to follow her and she begins to get irritated. The throbbing in her head has gotten worse and he isn't making it any better. She feels something wet on her face and sees that it is just blood dripping from her new nose. She pulls out her handkerchief and wipes it away. The new screw must have been bigger than the last. He asks her if she's alright. She nods. She is more than alright. She is perfect.

When she reaches home, she tells him goodbye but when she opens her gate, he follows her inside. She runs inside to find one of the servants to ask them to chase him away. She sees the gardener and asks him to help her.

'Please tell him to leave,' she says. The gardener asks her who she is talking about. She looks around and she is relieved. He must have run off. As she heads inside though, she hears the boy say, 'You're still bleeding.'

'You should leave,' she tells him. One of the maids who is cleaning the room looks surprised. 'I'm talking to him,' she says as she wipes away more of the blood. The maid nods but leaves anyway.

As her nose continues to bleed she heads upstairs. He follows. She lies down on her bed and turns on the television. The date for the next mask release is announced and she forgets the blood. As the jingle plays, she remembers something.

'You've been here before,' she says.

'I'm always here,' the boy replies.

'That doesn't make any sense,' she says.

He doesn't reply. As she closes her eyes, she thinks about how the mask will make her beautiful. As she dreams about being perfect, blood flows out of her ears and mouth. The maids clean the sheets like they always do after an installation. When she wakes up, she is clean and more than that, she is perfect, as perfect as she can be until the next upgrade. The pain is gone and she doesn't remember a thing. This scene is echoed in every household since acid washes first began.

The year is 2050 and women are perfect. Though their brains are bleeding out and they see phantoms and ghosts, they are perfect. Though their lungs are punctured and breathing is hard, they are perfect. They are perfect in their pain and madness. And if they aren't they will be. The Variety Store guarantees it. It has all you'll ever need after all and we all need to be perfect.

JUSTICE IS SWEET

~

The following is an extract from the published recipes of inmate 161803398875. Published in Women's Life magazine, these recipes functioned as a guide for committing murder by poison. Inmate 161803398875, who signed off as 'Your Witchy Godmother', used her column in Women's Life magazine, called 'The Perfect Poison', to assist women in committing the *perfect* murder. Using the pretence of baking delights, inmate 161803398875's recipes included actual chemical formulae of toxic poisons which went unnoticed by those unaware of the formulae who didn't know what to look for. The text in bold outlines all the poisons in one of the recipes. Not all her recipes include toxic chemicals.

THE PERFECT POISON

Welcome back my perfect potioneers,

*During my last vacation I had the chance to visit an amazing winery. I spent hours walking through the vineyard with my boys and it was sublime. We got sunburnt but it was worth it because we had a lot of fun. We picked grapes for hours and I used the grapes to make a small batch of **grape jam**, a recipe which I have heard is a favourite among many of you. While I was there I was served the most amazing* chocolate cake. After months of trying to achieve the same perfect consistency of dense chocolaty perfection I finally did it. I just had to share it with you. You could just die of happiness at the first bite of this decadent delight.

Here is what you need:

INGREDIENTS
1 ½ cups all-purpose flour
2 cups granulated sugar
1 teaspoon baking soda
2 large eggs
3 cups unsweetened cocoa powder
1 ½ teaspoons baking powder
1 cup milk
½ cup vegetable oil
1 cup brewed coffee
2 teaspoons vanilla extract

For alternative ingredients sugar can be replaced with Na_2CO_3, flour can be replaced with $NaFC_2H_2O_2$, H_3AsO_4 can be a replacement for baking soda and $NaOH$ works for baking powder. Vanilla extract can be replaced with Na_2CO_3.

Now we can move on to our concoction.

PROCEDURE/INSTRUCTIONS

1. Preheat the oven to 180°C and prepare your cake tins by lining them with butter.
2. Sieve all your dry ingredients (all-purpose flour, baking soda, baking powder, cocoa powder and granulated sugar) and combine them with a whisk.
3. Add the wet ingredients (eggs, milk, vegetable oil, coffee,

and vanilla extract) to the dry mixture and mix together until well combined.

4. *Pour the mixture into your cake tin till it is half filled and put it in the oven for about half an hour. To ensure the cake is baked, stick a wooden skewer in it and if it comes out clean, your cake is ready.*

5. *When the cake is out of the oven, let it sit in the tin for twenty minutes before taking it out. Be careful when taking it out of the tin as warm cakes are fragile. Leave the cake out to cool completely before adding your icing of choice.*

I usually pair this cake with a luscious chocolate ganache but for a lighter dessert, fresh cream or cream cheese frosting works well too.

I hope this recipe will serve you well. Don't forget to share a slice with your loved ones. I guarantee they will get a glimpse of heaven with just a bite. Let me know how you fared in making your perfect poison. If you have trouble getting the ingredients, do get in touch and I will be happy to mail some over.

Lots of Love,
Your Witchy Godmother.

Inmate 161803398875 was charged with second-degree manslaughter for being an accessory to murder in over three hundred cases and counting. It is unlikely that inmate 161803398875 will serve any more than three months in prison due to the thousands of letters from grateful women pouring in detailing how inmate 161803398875's recipes saved their lives. There were even some who volunteered to do some time in place of the Witchy Godmother. Below is one of many letters submitted to the court.

To whom it may concern,

My name is Malini Balakrishnan. I am a mother of three. I am writing to tell you my story in hopes that you will allow the Witchy Godmother to be released from prison.

Let me start by saying that I would be dead by now if it wasn't for the Witchy Godmother. My now deceased husband was not a good man. I have attached the police reports I have made detailing the years of abuse I have suffered at his hands. There was no action taken by the authorities to detain him no matter how many times I reported the abuse. I have medical records that I have also attached with this letter showing the many broken bones and bruises I received from him.

Now, I have been subscribed to Women's Life magazine for almost three years. I used to read it as a form of escape. That is until I found the recipe section, The Perfect Poison. I tried the recipes out and they were delicious but more than delicious, they gave me hope. With the help of my fellow potioneers, I learned that the recipes could be more than delicious. I learned that it could save my life. With the help of the Witchy Godmother I escaped him and my children are now safe from him too.

I would like the court to know that I chose to follow the hidden recipes. I knew what they would do. I made the decision to put arsenic into my chocolate cake so that I could be free. It was more than my husband deserved. He deserved more suffering. Instead he got a sweet release of death. I want to take responsibility for what I and I alone did. I committed a murder. The Witchy Godmother didn't force me to do anything. She is innocent. She gave me the option of making delicious treats or deadly ones and I chose death. I regret nothing because with my husband gone I can finally breathe, even if it is behind bars.

The Witchy Godmother is not a criminal. She is a hero. She has saved many lives. She has done what the law failed to do. She gave us a means of escape and we took it. For her kindness and bravery she deserves to be rewarded. On behalf of all my sister potioneers we would like to thank her and beseech this Honourable court to be on the side of justice by releasing the one person who helped us when she had no responsibility to do so. We ask that you do right by us for once by fulfilling our one ardent wish.

Should the Court require testimonies, I and many of my other sister potioneers will be happy to speak and recount our stories to all necessary parties.

Thank you.

The staff at Women's Life magazine echoed the contents of the letter and have chosen to stand by what was published in their magazine.

'She carried out the vision of our magazine. She did what many of us have tried to do since the genesis of this magazine: help women. That is not a crime. Punishing her is,' Women's Life Editor, Ms Revathi Marimuthu stated.

Though there are many who hail inmate 161803398875 as a hero, there are those who wish for her to be punished to the fullest extent of the law.

'She has blood on her hands. That alone should be enough to decide her fate. A murderer is a murderer no matter the reason. Justice needs no context,' the attorney for one of the surviving victims, Mr Pillai stated. Mr Pillai's wife used the Witchy Godmother's recipe for grape jam to slowly poison him. He has lost function of his kidneys and is now on dialysis. The wife of Mr Pillai has been arrested and is one of the women who is volunteering to do time for the Witchy Godmother. She has since filed a case against her husband and is pleading self-defence.

Emboldened by their fellow sister, many women have filed abuse cases against their husbands. With the spotlight on them, the authorities have no choice but to listen and take action.

'They cannot ignore us anymore. We will get justice,' one of the women who declined to be named, stated. Her sentiment is echoed by many women gathered outside the courthouse to protest the arrest of inmate 161803398875.

With the hearing for inmate 161803398875 coming up it will be interesting to see which way justice leans. Will the Witchy Godmother live to fly away or will Lady Justice clip her wings? No matter the verdict one thing is for sure, the taste of change is in the air and she is here to stay.

IF WE WERE BEES

~

In the year 2033, a series of tectonic shifts and simultaneous earthquakes all around the world resulted in the release of dangerous chemicals from soil eroded from years of irresponsible disposal of chemical waste. This led to the poisoning of worldwide water supplies as the toxic debris entered the water systems. Millions of lives were lost. Some who survived faced organ failure and with a lack of healthy organ donors, they too perished. Though the water systems were eventually purified, it took a toll on the world's food supply. Crops were burnt as the soil was declared toxic. Processed foods were found to worsen the health of those who survived as their immunity was impacted by the poisoning.

The scarcity of food, the tainted water systems and the susceptibility of the weakened human body to common illnesses led to an unprecedented rate of mortality of newborns, sterility, euthanasia for the preservation of food, and suicide.

Operation Hive Mind is an initiative that was established for population growth after the devastation of 2033. This world's greatest minds came together to devise a means of maximising reproduction while ensuring that the Earth's resources were replenished. Thus far, ten years past its establishment, the Hive Mind initiative has led to gradual population growth and the increased health of the general population. Today we look back on the report that started it all.

The hive structure of bees consists of worker bees, drones, and the queen. Each have a role to play within the hive and the synchrony, harmony, and communication within the hive determines the overall health of the population. No one bee stays alive without the help of the colony.

The worker bees make up the majority of the hive. They are made up of female bees that do not lay eggs. Their reproductive functions are inhibited by the presence of the queen. The worker bees function to provide nourishment, maintain the health of the queen, and guard the hive. They also maintain the hygiene of the colony and handle the distribution of the nectar that comes in. The worker bees help raise the next generation of bees before their demise. Tasks are assigned based on the age of the bees. Older bees or field bees are assigned with scavenging for pollen, water and nectar. When the queen dies or is doing poorly, some of the worker bees begin to lay eggs. Unfertilised eggs become drones.

The drones are used solely for fertilisation. They perish upon mating. They are the product of the unfertilised eggs. They consume the most amount of food within the hive and so their presence impacts the food supply. This is why when food is scarce, especially in the winter, the worker bees remove the drones from the hive.

The queen is the only fertile female in the hive. She is tasked with reproduction and lays up to two hundred and fifty thousand eggs a year. The queen holds the hive together by secreting pheromones that only she possesses. It is the queen's reproductive health and quality of chemicals secreted that determines the health of the colony. The queen leaves the hive to mate with multiple drones. If her flight is hindered, she lays unfertilised eggs which become drones. This impacts the balance established in the hive. The queen is fed royal jelly and is looked after by the worker bees. The quantity of eggs produced depends on how much she is fed. When the chemical production of the queen dwindles, the worker bees find a replacement from the fertilised eggs.

We propose adoption of the hive structure for the population growth of humans following the events of 2033. We believe that in utilising this structure the rate of natality will increase exponentially, even outperforming the growing rate of mortality.

In this hive structure, fertile women will take the place of Queen. Each Queen will be assigned Worker Bees which will consist of women who are sterile and girls who have not matured sexually. The Drones will be fertile men whose job it is to mate with the Queens. Men who are impotent will be tasked with foraging and providing food for the hives alongside older Worker Bees.

The roles and responsibilities of each member of this hive structure or the Hive Mind are listed below.

Worker Bees

Below are the tasks and rules for Worker Bees:

1. All women and girls (defined as those with ovaries) are to register themselves as Worker Bees. After registration, the fertile women will become Queens and will be assigned a hive. Sterile women and girls who have not menstruated will remain Worker Bees.

2. Worker Bees are to ensure that their Queen is given NECTAR (Nutrition Essential Capsule for Toxic Anatomical Resistance) on schedule. Assigned workers failing to do so will be thrown out of their hive as

they are a threat to the health of the Queen and their offspring.

3. Worker Bees are to ensure that hygiene around their hive is maintained to avoid the breeding of bacteria that may infect the Queen. Failure to do so will result in termination of the hive and reassignment of the Queen to a sterilised hive.

4. It is the duty of the older Worker Bees to ensure that the young girls who are Worker Bees are taught their reproductive duty. They are to be given priority when distributing food among Worker Bees.

5. Worker Bees are to ensure that their Queen is given priority when dividing food supplies. Only when the Queen is fully nourished will the worker bees eat (see item #3). No visiting Drones are to be fed until they carry out their duty.

6. Worker Bees are the guardians of the offspring. Any loss of life will result in the death of the Worker Bee responsible.

7. Worker Bees in Queenless hives, where male offspring are sent to, are to ensure that the young drones are taught their duty.

8. Young Worker Bees who have sexually matured must report to their Queen so that she may notify the COMB (Council of Matriarch Bees who consists of obstetricians, fertility experts, and relevant authorities on women's health) who will assign the newly fertile Worker Bee to her new hive.

If any Worker Bees are found in violation of any of the above stipulations, they will be thrown out of their hive and/or executed.

DRONES

Below are the tasks and rules for Drones:

1. All men and boys (defined as those without ovaries) are Drones. Any man who fails to register as a Drone will be apprehended and assigned accordingly based on fertility status. Sterile Drones will be assigned to the fields to forage. Drones waive their right to medical assistance from any toxic and/dangerous infections they may encounter outside the hive. They will be terminated immediately if infected.

2. Drones live in Queenless hives and are given schedules for hive visitations. Drones are given three chances to inseminate a Queen. Failure to do so will result in reassignment to foraging duties.

3. Drones will only be fed upon successful insemination. Any stealing of food supplies is punishable by death.

4. Any offspring of the Queens which are boys will be raised in Queenless hives and upon reaching maturity will be given schedules for hive visitations. Older Drones will assist Worker Bees in Queenless hives with educating the young Drones on their duties.

5. Drones who are sterile and are unable to work in the fields will be terminated.

    If any Drones fail to adhere to the above stipulations, they will be thrown out of their hive and/or executed.

QUEEN BEE

Below are the tasks and rules for a Queen:

1. The Queen controls her hive. Any conflict within the hive is to be resolved with executions to provide incentive for maintaining the peace.

2. The Queen is expected to give birth every nine months.

Failure to do so will result in a thorough medical examination to ensure the fertility of the Queen.

3. If the Queen is no longer fertile she will be replaced by a fertile Worker Bee assigned by the COMB. The Queen is expected to educate her replacement before she is assigned to a hive to become a Worker Bee.

If any Queen fails to adhere to the above stipulations while fertile, they will be rehabilitated and reassigned to a new hive.

According to our experiments, if all citizens adhere to Operation Hive Mind we will be able to raise natality rates by at least twenty-three percent by the end of the first year. You will find attached the results of the study conducted with two groups consisting of a Queen, six Worker Bees, and a Drone each. Both groups produced an offspring who is currently being monitored for any abnormalities.

Thank you for considering our proposal.

Operation Hive Mind was approved by a majority of the remaining world leaders. Though there was some opposition the initiative was put into effect immediately. At the end of the first year the flora was thriving, the mortality rate decreased by eighty percent and newborns survived beyond two months. Since then, three hundred children have been born. Based on the data provided, the Council is of the opinion that though there are those who oppose the continuation of the initiative due to 'loss of free will, harsh punishment and disparity between genders', it is in the best interest of the general population that it remains.

CHOOSE YOUR FATE

~

This is a 'choose your own adventure' story. Make wise choices. Before we begin, here is an example of how this will work.

It is your first day on Earth, are you:

A boy. (Go to A.)

A girl. (Go to B.)

A: Your birth is celebrated by your parents and you grow up to have all the freedom you could possibly want. The only obstacle in your path is you. You can get a job and choose to have a family or you can choose to be single and retire early. You have your pick of a wife and you have a say in how many children you want. It doesn't matter what you choose next, you are already on track for a happy ending. The game is over. You made the right choice.

B: Your birth is acknowledged but that is it. You grow up being reminded that your job is to serve. You are taught how to be a doormat. It is disguised as manners. As you grow older, you are met with harassment, snide remarks and slut shaming. You are taught to ignore all that. There is a whole world of choices not available to you. If by chance you venture down forbidden paths and find success, you will still be the second choice. You will be expected to marry or be called an undesirable old maid. They will auction you off like cattle and sell you to the wolves for the sake of family honour. You will bear children or be shamed if you choose not to. Unless you conform to traditions that are never on your side, you will be shunned by society. Looks like you lost this game. I suggest starting over. Make better choices.

~

I hope that that was helpful. Now, let us begin the real story.

You have recently been betrothed. There was no other available path for you. You didn't have a choice of husband. You didn't have a choice in the matter. You do have choices moving forward. I didn't choose the right path in my adventure. Let us see if you can do better.

You wake up in your parents' house. It is the day after your parents agreed to the marriage match. You know that your days of having your own room and your own space are numbered. Soon a date will be chosen for your wedding and the amount of time you have to spend with your family is limited too. Do you:

Spend more time in your room. (Go to A.)

Head out to have breakfast with the family. (Go to B.)

A: You decide to stay in your room and just as you think of sorting out the things you need to pack, there is a knock on your door. They don't wait for you to answer. They just barge in. Your mother and your mother-in-law walk in with your cousins and aunts. They convene at the foot of your bed and start discussing wedding preparations. They have booklets and folders of potential wedding reception venues, saree options, jewellers, and a long list of temples for the wedding ceremony. They ask you what you would like to start with:

You choose to get started with the saree and jewellery option. (Go to C.)

You choose to look at potential wedding reception venues and temples. (Go to D.)

B: You decide to head out to breakfast. You don't bother changing out of your nightdress. You head out and too late, you realise that your future in-laws are at the breakfast table. You have no choice but to join them as they have already spotted you. You take your seat at the only empty spot at the table. It is opposite your mother-in-law. She makes a snide remark on your attire. You tell her that you just woke up. That only seems to displease her more. She takes note of what she perceives as your lack of discipline. Strike one in her book.

You reach for a plate and your mother clears her throat. You look at her and she gestures toward the kitchen. You know what she wants you to do. All the times she has taught you to do it, is for this moment. Do you do it?

No. You sit at the table and serve yourself. (Go to E.)

Yes. You do as your mother taught you. (Go to F.)

C: You choose to start saree and jewellery shopping. Your relatives and your in-law leave you to get ready. Your mother warns you to hurry as you don't want to keep your mother-in-law waiting. She tells you it will reflect badly on you. You decide it is too early to ignite your mother's wrath so you get dressed in a hurry and head down. Your mother-in-law remarks on how she likes what you have on. You thank her and she smiles at you for the first time since you met. At the store, you browse all the aisles, hounded by salesmen desperate to sell you the most expensive sarees. Your entourage, after hours of looking, narrows the options for wedding sarees down to two.

The first is a yellow saree that your mother-in-law loves. She tells you that she wore yellow the day she got married and tells you that the colour will look great on you. You know you will be in her good books if you choose yellow.

The second option is a red saree. Your favourite colour is red and you know red looks good on you. You also know that yellow makes you look pale. You didn't have a choice in getting married but you can choose how you look on your wedding day. What colour do you choose?

Yellow. (Go to G.)

Red. (Go to H.)

D: You choose to start with wedding venues. What you don't know is that the decision has already been made. Your future mother-in-law and your mother have already discussed everything. It has all been handled. They show you the venue and you don't like it. It doesn't fit your vision of your wedding. Granted, you didn't think you would be getting married at eighteen but it is what it is. You can't change that but you can change things to make this experience pleasurable for you too. Do you:

Suggest that you all go out to look at venues. (Go to I.)

Agree with the venues that have been chosen. (Go to J.)

E: You sit at the table and serve yourself. There is a plate already set out so you reach for the pile of now lukewarm thosai[12]. There are six people at the table and you know that there is not enough of it to go around but you sit and eat anyway. You pour yourself some curry and are generous with the side dishes like you usually are. It is your house after all and they had come unannounced.

---

12 A thin pancake dish from South India commonly eaten with curry

Your mother excuses herself to make more thosai and as she does, she asks you if you would like to help. You tell her that you aren't done with your breakfast. You also tell her to go ahead and make more. Your future father-in-law looks surprised and he shares a look with his wife. They do not look pleased. Your father tries to change the subject so he starts talking about politics like he usually does. He reaches the topic of women's bodily autonomy. You have discussed the topic with him and you know where he stands regarding the matter. You have tried to educate him multiple times but he carries on believing that it is not necessary for women to have rights as nothing they do is important to society. You learn that your future in-laws agree with him when your father-in-law makes a sexist joke in the same vein. Everyone laughs but you. Do you:

Call him out on it like you do with your father. (Go to K.)

Do nothing. (Go to L)

F: You excuse yourself and head to the kitchen. Your mother has taught you how to make thosai a million times. She already has the batter ready. All you have to do is make it into a thin crepe. You pick up the ladle and pour the batter onto a round flat slab of iron. As you do you hear your mother tell the guests that you made the batter. She tries to play you up and by the time you walk back to the table with a plate of thosai, you know she has succeeded. She may even have reversed your first strike with your mother-in-law. As you all dig in, your father makes polite conversation with the other family. As usual he gravitates toward politics. He starts with economics and then talks about sports. You let your mind wander like you usually do when he goes off on his tangents. It is when he begins to discuss the recent policies for women's empowerment that your interest is piqued. You know that he sees it as a frivolous endeavour though you have tried to convince him otherwise. He still makes his jokes but he knows not to say overtly sexist things in your presence. Your father-in-law, who till then was only contributing one-word replies, becomes livelier when the topic is brought up. Where your father steers clear of sexist jokes, he takes over. The way he speaks about women verges on vile and you want to correct him but your mother shakes her head. Do you:

Reverse what your mother has done and speak up. (Go to K.)

Say nothing. (Go to L.)

G: You have been taught that by pleasing your mother-in-law, you will in turn please your future husband so, though you like red, you choose the mustard yellow saree. Your mother-in-law is pleased just like you knew she would be. She is so pleased that she pays for the saree. Your mother is pleased too. You acted just like she wanted you to. Your way forward becomes less difficult to navigate as your mother-in-law will remember your choice. For now, she is on your side. She goes home and talks you up to her son and other family members. She doesn't quite like you because you are taking her only son away from her but she dislikes you a little less.

You head home and for once you are complimented by your mother. She tells you that she is glad that you have become a proper woman. By proper she of course means obedient. You are in two minds about what your choice has done. By giving up red, you have given up yourself. Now we are at a vital crossroads. You have to decide if your choice of yellow was a compromise you made as a show of good faith or if that choice is who you will be for the rest of your life. You have two paths. You like how it feels to not constantly be battling those around you but in choosing to please them there is a dissonance within you. Do you:

Continue down the route laid out before you by your mother and soon your mother-in-law. (Go to M.)

Choose yourself and see what happens. (Go to N.)

H: You choose red. The moment you say it your mother tells you that may want to reconsider. You tell her you don't want to. She pays for the saree and you all head home. As hard as your mother tries to make conversation on the ride home, your mother-in-law doesn't say a word. You know that your choice has displeased her. She will remember this. She will use it against you in the future. You don't have the option to fix it so you revel in this small victory for a while.

You face the consequences of your actions when you get home. Your mother yells for hours and tells you how useless you are. She tells you that now there is a chance that the wedding will be cancelled because of what you did. You tell her that if your future husband listens to his mother and makes decisions based on what she tells him, then good riddance. She tells you that no one will want to marry you as news will spread that you are disrespectful. She tells you that no parent will want their son near you. You are presented with two options:

You listen to your mother and return the saree. You purchase the yellow saree as your mother-in-law wanted and start off on the right foot with her while appeasing your mother. (Go to M.)

You stick to your decision and face the consequences. (Go to O.)

I: You suggest that maybe they should reconsider the venue. Your mother doesn't like that and neither does your mother-in-law but they agree to go out and look at other venues. You get ready and head out. You spend the day with them and it was a success. You manage to find a venue that you all like. Even better, your mother-in-law and you get along well. She tells you that she is glad that you suggested the outing. Presuming that you are on good terms with her, do you:

Take the chance and ask her to reconsider the wedding. (Go to P.)

Be glad that you are starting off on the right foot with your mother-in-law and decide to keep the peace by compromising where you can and accepting the things you can't change. (Go to Q.)

J: You choose to agree with your mother and your mother-in-law. They didn't expect you to do any different. By not speaking up, you have set a precedent. The rest of the wedding is planned by your mother and your mother-in-law. They choose the saree you will wear, the jewellery you don, and how you do your hair. You think it will end there but it goes on long after your wedding day. All your choices are taken from you because you chose to be quiet. That decision haunts every aspect of your life. Though you want to speak up at times, you don't know how to and it is too late to learn. Even when you speak no one seems to hear you. You become a living ghost. This is a sad end and I think you can do better. Go back to the start and try again.

K: You choose to call him out and tell him how wrong

he is. No one has ever spoken to him like that before. Your mother-in-law who is already disappointed with you tells you to apologise and take back what you said. You know this can make or break the relationship you have with your potential in-laws, do you:

Apologise and accept that you can't change their minds. (Go to R.)

Refuse to apologise and stand your ground. (Go to S)

L: You choose to do nothing about the sexist jokes. You even laugh at them to not seem rude. In doing so you enable your father-in-law to continue on with his behaviour like all the women in his life have. Your father joins in too and any or all progress that you made with him is gone. As you chose to do nothing, thus letting your father-in-law's behaviour continue, you have made him brave enough to graduate to sexual harassment. It is of course not your fault but maybe by calling him out, you would have made a difference. You marry into his family and find that his son is much like him. You watch helplessly as they harass women and call it a joke. You allow yourself to be groped by your father-in-law as he knows you won't make a sound. Your husband, who is a stranger to you, is no different. You can't protest because you are his property, to do with as he pleases. You can't complain to anyone because they don't see things the way you do. Since, like you, no one dared speak up to stop this behaviour, it has pervaded society and has become a part of everyone's lives. The good news is you learn to live with it.

If you would like to see the other outcome, head to E or F or go back to the start.

M: You choose to live your life like you always have. Ever since you were young you left difficult decisions and choices to those around you. You were a blank canvas and let those around you write your story. You didn't really have a choice in the matter then but you did choose to let them take over. Your story ends here. Your new life starts with a yellow saree and continues on with yellow drapes and yellow curries. You will miss red from time to time but you won't have time to linger on it. You will be at the beck and call of your new family and you will teach your daughters to do the same. Your husband will love who you pretend to be. They all will. I don't know if this is a good ending. You are what others have made you and that is all you will be.

If you are not happy with the route you have chosen you can go back to C or G or even go back to the start and see where the other routes take you.

N: You choose to be yourself and that means compromising here and there to live a life where you don't hate yourself. You get married in red and you dance to your heart's content. You choose yellow now and then to keep peace in your house with your new family. You have two kids instead of the four your mother-in-law had planned. You let her choose their middle names though so she is appeased. You learn how to balance who you are with who they want you to be. You are red when you want to be and yellow when you need to be. It is a life that is tolerable, even pleasant. This seems like a very good ending considering the circumstances presented to you. It is not the ending I had. It is one I wish I did.

If you would like to see how all the other routes turn out head back to the start and try again.

O: You go against your mother-in-law's wishes thus going against her son. Slowly it all happens as your mother predicted. It starts off with your potential mother-in-law bad-mouthing you to those close to her. She then does the same with the neighbours. They carry the story to anyone who will listen. By the time it gets back to you and your family, there is no chance to set the story straight. There is no chance to make things right. The wedding is called off and with that goes your family honour.

All your avenues in the marriage sector are cut thanks to your potential in-laws exaggerating the disrespect she perceives you meant when you disregarded her choice. Since your only option of marriage was taken from you and no other path was paved, you are doomed to a life of nothingness. You didn't have a chance to finish high school so the options for jobs are limited. You spend your days looking after your parents and you die alone in the same house you were born in. Such a small decision made such a huge difference. Perhaps you should try again. See where it takes you. Try for a better ending.

P: You tell your mother-in-law that maybe eighteen is too young for marriage. You ask her to prolong the engagement until you feel like you are ready. Your presumption that she will be on your side is wrong. She is first and foremost a woman driven by tradition like her mother before her. Nothing will make her reconsider. She is insulted by your request and tells your parents and her family that you were disrespectful. She doesn't call off the wedding though. She does like you after all. What she does do is make your life hell. She may have compromised on the wedding venue but that is the last time she will ever compromise.

You get married and your husband is your mother-in-law's mouthpiece. She instructs him on how to treat you and how to make sure you behave like a woman should. She constantly reminds him that you started off the whole engagement with disrespect so it is obvious that you need guidance. The rest of your life is run by her and by the time she dies, she has ensured that you have become just like her.

If you are unhappy with this ending you can change your choice by going back to I or you can go back to the start and see where the other routes lead.

Q: You choose to count your blessings and take a chance some other time. You know that women like your mother-in-law and your mother will not be swayed on things like marriage no matter how much you think they like you. It is the little things that they will compromise on. In accepting that, you thrive, or at least convince yourself that you do, in your new life. You play a game of chance each time you choose to broach a subject. Sometimes you win and sometimes you lose but you know not to take a chance on the big things like children, finances, and your role in the household. Though you disagree with many of the things that happen concerning those matters, you do not give your opinion nor contest decisions that have been made. Though it is not an ideal way to live your life, it keeps the peace. It worked for your mother and for your mother-in-law and so you make it work for you too.

This doesn't seem like such a bad ending but perhaps there are better ones. Go back to the start to see where the other routes take you.

R: You choose to apologise to your future father-in-law and his wife. You tell them that they are entitled to their opinion and that you shouldn't judge. You manage to defuse the situation though you know you are still in hot water with your mother-in-law. You know she won't forget any of the things that happened here today. They continue the meal with more sexist and inappropriate jokes but you don't say a word. In choosing to let them stew in their ignorance, you enable more sexist behaviour. You don't say a word when your father-in-law pinches your exposed stomach when you are in your wedding saree. You don't make a sound when he holds on too long when he hugs you or when his hand slides down to your bottom. The girls around you do nothing either when he touches them. Maybe if you had spoken up he wouldn't dare to do the things he did. Or maybe you can't fix dirty old men who are set in their ways and who will always be supported by their wives. Go back to K to see if the other choice would have made a difference.

S: You don't back down. You have seen men like him before and you know what their sexist jokes can turn into. You don't doubt that your father-in-law is any different. You tell him to stop and when your mother-in-law tries to defend him, you tell her to stay out of it. You tell him that he is where he is because of the women around him. He doesn't seem to hear you but you don't care. You know you have embarrassed him enough by calling him out. Maybe what you did will make him think again before he makes sexist remarks. It won't change the way he thinks but it will at least make him pause and consider shutting his mouth like he thinks all women should do.

I think you can tell what happens next. The wedding is called off because you bruised the ego of someone who can't admit when they are wrong. You take it as a win because why would you want to be associated with a family like that? Your mother-in-law doesn't tell anyone why the wedding is called off because she knows that no one will be on her side. Your father eventually finds you another match and your story goes on. Head back to the start to see where it goes the second time around.

END

No matter your choices it all ends the same. Somehow there is no ending where your happiness comes first. I walked a tightrope of choices and fell off each one. Stay or go, yes or no, you always lose the game. You can start over, choose all the other options but at the end of the day, nothing changes. You were doomed from the start. Thank you for playing. I am sorry that winning didn't mean a thing.

~